Ursula Kroeber Le Guin is indisputably one of the greatest science fiction writers of our time. Born in California in 1929, her outstanding contribution to the SF field has all been made during the last ten years. Since her work first appeared in print in 1961, she has won the prestigious Hugo Award four times and the Nebula Award three times: *The Left Hand of Darkness* (Nebula in 1969 and Hugo in 1970), *The Word for World is Forest* (Hugo in 1973), *The Ones Who Walk Away from Omelas* (Hugo in 1974), *The Day Before the Revolution* (Nebula in 1974), and *The Dispossessed* which won a Nebula in 1974, the year of its publication, and a Hugo in 1975.

The Wind's Twelve Quarters:
'Her worlds are strange, moody, fantastic, eerie places . . . her heroes are stretched to the limits of endurance as they face every possible mental and physical threat which a fertile imagination can produce.'
The Scotsman

'Some writers consistently ride the peaks . . . Ursula Le Guin is one.'
Birmingham Post

Also by Ursula Le Guin

Rocannon's World
Planet of Exile
City of Illusions
The Left Hand of Darkness
A Wizard of Earthsea
The Tombs of Atuan
The Farthest Shore
The Lathe of Heaven
The Dispossessed
The Wind's Twelve Quarters (Vol. 1)
Orsinian Tales

Ursula Le Guin

The Wind's Twelve Quarters
Volume II

PANTHER
GRANADA PUBLISHING
London Toronto Sydney New York

Published by Granada Publishing Limited
in Panther Books 1978, 1980

ISBN 0 586 04623 2

First published in Great Britain in one volume under
the title of *The Wind's Twelve Quarters* by
Victor Gollancz Ltd, 1976
Copyright © Ursula K. Le Guin 1975

Things originally appeared under the title *The End* in *Orbit 6*, 1970
A Trip to the Head originally appeared in *Quark 1* 1970
Vaster than Empires and More Slow originally appeared in
 New Dimensions 1, 1971
The Stars Below originally appeared in *Orbit 12*, 1973
The Field of Vision originally appeared in *Galaxy*, 1973
Direction of the Road originally appeared in *Orbit 14*, 1974
The Ones Who Walk Away from Omelas originally appeared in *New Dimensions
 3*, 1973
The Day Before the Revolution originally appeared in *Galaxy*, 1974

Granada Publishing Limited
Frogmore, St Albans, Herts AL2 2NF
and
3 Upper James Street, London W1R 4BP
866 United Nations Plaza, New York, NY 10017, USA
117 York Street, Sydney, NSW 2000, Australia
100 Skyway Avenue, Rexdale, Ontario, M9W 3A6, Canada
PO Box 84165, Greenside, 2034 Johannesburg, South Africa
CML Centre, Queen & Wyndham, Auckland 1, New Zealand

Set, printed and bound in Great Britain by
Cox & Wyman Ltd, Reading
Set in Intertype Plantin

Granada ®
Granada Publishing ®

Contents

Things 7

A Trip to the Head 18

Vaster than Empires and More Slow 25

The Stars Below 60

The Field of Vision 82

Direction of the Road 105

The Ones who Walk Away from Omelas 112

The Day Before the Revolution 121

THINGS

Damon Knight, editor mirabilis, first published this story in a volume of Orbit, *under the title 'The End'. I don't now remember how we arrived at it, but I suspect he thought that 'Things' sounded too much like something you see on the television at one* A.M., *with purple tentacles. But I have gone back to it because – at least after reading the psychomyth – it puts the right emphasis. Things you use; things you possess, and are possessed by; things you build with – bricks, words. You build houses with them, and towns, and causeways. But the buildings fall, the causeways cannot go all the way. There is an abyss, a gap, a last step to be taken.*

On the shore of the sea he stood looking out over the long foam-lines far where vague the Islands lifted or were guessed. There, he said to the sea, there lies my kingdom. The sea said to him what the sea says to everybody. As evening moved from behind his back across the water the foam-lines paled and the wind fell, and very far in the west shone a star perhaps, perhaps a light, or his desire for a light.

He climbed the streets of his town again in late dusk. The shops and huts of his neighbors were looking empty now, cleared out, cleaned up, packed away in preparation for the end. Most of the people were up at the Weeping in Heights-Hall or down with the Ragers in the fields. But Lif had not been able to clear out and clean up; his wares and belongings were too heavy to throw away, too hard to break, too dull to burn. Only centuries could waste them. Wherever they were piled or dropped or thrown they formed what might have been, or

seemed to be, or yet might be, a city. So he had not tried to get rid of his things. His yard was still stacked and piled with bricks, thousands and thousands of bricks of his own making. The kiln stood cold but ready, the barrels of clay and dry mortar and lime, the hods and barrows and trowels of his trade, everything was there. One of the fellows from Scriveners Lane had asked sneering, Going to build a brick wall and hide behind it when that old end comes, man?

Another neighbor on his way up to the Heights-Hall gazed a while at those stacks and heaps and loads and mounds of well-shaped, well-baked bricks all a soft reddish gold in the gold of the afternoon sun, and sighed at last with the weight of them on his heart: Things, things! Free yourself of things, Lif, from the weight that drags you down! Come with us, above the ending world!

Lif had picked up a brick from the heap and put it in place on the stack and smiled in embarrassment. When they were all past he had gone neither up to the Hall nor out to help wreck the fields and kill the animals, but down to the beach, the end of the ending world, beyond which lay only water. Now back in his brickyard hut with the smell of salt in his clothes and his face hot with the sea wind, he still felt neither the Ragers' laughing and wrecking despair nor the soaring and weeping despair of the communicants of the Heights; he felt empty; he felt hungry. He was a heavy little man and the sea wind at the world's edge had blown at him all evening without moving him at all.

Hey Lif! said the widow from Weavers Lane, which crossed his street a few houses down, —I saw you coming up the street, and never another soul since sunset, and getting dark, and quieter than ... She did not say what the town was quieter than, but went on, Have you had your supper? I was about to take my roast out of the oven, and the little one and I will never eat up all that meat before the end comes, no doubt, and I hate to see good meat go to waste.

Well thank you very much, says Lif, putting on his coat

again; and they went down Masons Lane to Weavers Lane
through the dark and the wind sweeping up steep streets from
the sea. In the widow's lamplit house Lif played with her
baby, the last born in the town, a little fat boy just learning how
to stand up. Lif stood him up and he laughed and fell over,
while the widow set out bread and hot meat on the table of
heavy woven cane. They sat to eat, even the baby, who worked
with four teeth at a hard hunk of bread. —How is it you're not
up on the Hill or in the fields? asked Lif, and the widow
replied as if the answer sufficed to her mind, Oh, I have the
baby.

Lif looked around the little house which her husband, who
had been one of Lif's bricklayers, had built. —This is good, he
said. I haven't tasted meat since last year some time.

I know, I know! No houses being built any more.

Not a one, he said. Not a wall nor a henhouse, not even
repairs. But your weaving, that's still wanted?

Yes; some of them want new clothes right up to the end.
This meat I bought from the Ragers that slaughtered all my
lord's flocks, and I paid with the money I got for a piece of fine
linen I wove for my lord's daughter's gown that she wants to
wear at the end! The widow gave a little derisive, sympathetic
snort, and went on: But now there's no flax, and scarcely any
wool. No more to spin, no more to weave. The fields burnt and
the flocks dead.

Yes, said Lif, eating the good roast meat. Bad times, he said,
the worst times.

And now, the widow went on, where's bread to come from,
with the fields burnt? And water, now they're poisoning the
wells? I sound like the Weepers up there, don't I? Help your-
self, Lif. Spring lamb's the finest meat in the world, my man
always said, till autumn came and then he'd say roast pork's the
finest meat in the world. Come on now, give yourself a proper
slice . . .

That night in his hut in the brickyard Lif dreamed. Usually
he slept as still as the bricks themselves but this night he drifted

and floated in dream all night to the Islands, and when he woke they were no longer a wish or a guess: like a star as daylight darkens they had become certain, he knew them. But what, in his dream, had borne him over the water? He had not flown, he had not walked, he had not gone underwater like the fish; yet he had come across the grey-green plains and wind-moved hillocks of the sea to the Islands, he had heard voices call, and seen the lights of towns.

He set his mind to think how a man could ride on water. He thought of how grass floats on streams, and saw how one might make a sort of mat of woven cane and lie on it pushing with one's hands: but the great canebrakes were still smoldering down by the stream, and the piles of withies at the basketmaker's had all been burnt. On the Islands in his dream he had seen canes or grasses half a hundred feet high, with brown stems thicker than his arms could reach round, and a world of green leaves spread sunward from the thousand outreaching twigs. On those stems a man might ride over the sea. But no such plants grew in his country nor ever had; though in the Heights-Hall was a knife-handle made of a dull brown stuff, said to come from a plant that grew in some other land, called wood. But he could not ride across the bellowing sea on a knife-handle.

Greased hides might float; but the tanners had been idle now for weeks, there were no hides for sale. He might as well stop looking about for any help. He carried his barrow and his largest hod down to the beach that white windy morning and laid them in the still water of a lagoon. Indeed they floated, deep in the water, but when he leaned even the weight of one hand on them they tipped, filled, sank. They were too light, he thought.

He went back up the cliff and through the streets, loaded the barrow with useless well-made bricks, and wheeled a hard load down. As so few children had been born these last years there was no young curiosity about to ask him what he was doing, though a Rager or two, groggy from last night's wreckfest, glanced sidelong at him from a dark doorway through the

brightness of the air. All that day he brought down bricks and
the makings of mortar, and the next day, though he had not had
the dream again, he began to lay his bricks there on the blus-
tering beach of March with rain and sand handy in great quan-
tities to set his cement. He built a little brick dome, upside
down, oval with pointed ends like a fish, all of a single course of
bricks laid spiral very cunningly. If a cupful or a barrowful of
air would float, would not a brick domeful? And it would be
strong. But when the mortar was set, and straining his broad
back he overturned the dome and pushed it into the cream of
the breakers, it dug deeper and deeper into the wet sand, bur-
rowing down like a clam or a sand flea. The waves filled it, and
refilled it when he tipped it empty, and at last a green-shoul-
dered breaker caught it with its white dragging backpull, rolled
it over, smashed it back into its elemental bricks and sank them
in the restless sodden sand. There stood Lif wet to the neck and
wiping salt spray out of his eyes. Nothing lay westward on the
sea but wavewrack and rainclouds. But they were there. He
knew them, with their great grasses ten times a man's height,
their wild golden fields raked by the sea wind, their white
towns, their white-crowned hills above the sea; and the voices
of shepherds called on the hills.

I'm a builder, not a floater, said Lif after he had considered
his stupidity from all sides. And he came doggedly out of the
water and up the cliff-side path and through the rainy streets to
get another barrowload of bricks.

Free for the first time in a week for his fool dream of
floating, he noticed now that Leather Street seemed deserted.
The tannery was rubbishy and vacant. The craftsmen's shops
lay like a row of little black gaping mouths, and the sleeping-
room windows above them were blind. At the end of the lane an
old cobbler was burning, with a terrible stench, a small heap of
new shoes never worn. Beside him a donkey waited, saddled,
flicking its ears at the stinking smoke.

Lif went on and loaded his barrow with bricks. This time as
he wheeled it down, straining back against the tug of the

barrow on the steep streets, swinging all the strength of his shoulders to balance its course on the winding cliff-path down to the beach, a couple of townsmen followed him. Two or three more from Scriveners Lane followed after them, and several more from the streets round the market place, so that by the time he straightened up, the sea foam fizzing on his bare black feet and the sweat cold on his face, there was a little crowd strung out along the deep single track of his barrow over the sand. They had the lounging listless air of Ragers. Lif paid them no heed, though he was aware that the widow of Weavers Lane was up on the cliffs watching with a scared face.

He ran the barrow out into the sea till the water was up to his chest, and tipped the bricks out, and came running in with a great breaker, his banging barrow full of foam.

Already some of the Ragers were drifting away down the beach. A tall fellow from the Scriveners Lane lot lounged by him and said with a little grin, Why don't you throw 'em from the top of the cliff, man?

They'd only hit the sand, said Lif.

And you want to drown 'em. Well good. You know there was some of us thought you was building something down here! They was going to make cement out of you. Keep those bricks wet and cool, man.

Grinning, the Scrivener drifted off, and Lif started up the cliff for another load.

Come for supper, Lif, said the widow at the cliff's top with a worried voice, holding her baby close to keep it from the wind.

I will, he said. I'll bring a loaf of bread, I laid in a couple before the bakers left. He smiled, but she did not. As they climbed the streets together she asked, Are you dumping your bricks in the sea, Lif?

He laughed wholeheartedly and answered yes.

She had a look then that might have been relief and might have been sadness; but at supper in her lamplit house she was quiet and easy as ever, and they ate their cheese and stale bread with good cheer.

Next day he went on carrying bricks down load after load, and if the Ragers watched him they thought him busy on their own kind of work. The slope of the beach out to deep water was gradual, so that he could keep building without ever working above water. He had started at low tide so that his work would never be laid bare. At high tide it was hard, dumping the bricks and trying to lay them in rough courses with the whole sea boiling in his face and thundering over his head, but he kept at it. Towards evening he brought down long iron rods and braced what he had built, for a crosscurrent tended to undermine his causeway about eight feet from its beginning. He made sure that even the tips of the rods were under water at low tide, so that no Rager might suspect an affirmation was being made. A couple of elderly men coming down from a Weeping in the Heights-Hall passed him clanging and battering his empty barrow up the stone streets in dusk, and gravely smiled upon him. It is well to be free of Things, said one softly, and the other nodded.

Next day, though still he had not dreamed of the Islands again, Lif went on building his causeway. The sand began to shelve off more steeply as he went further. His method now was to stand on the last bit he had built and tip the carefully-loaded barrow from there, and then tip himself off and work, floundering and gasping and coming up and pushing down, to get the bricks levelled and fitted between the pre-set rods; then up again, across the grey sand and up the cliff and bang-clatter through the quiet streets for another load.

Some time that week the widow said, meeting him in his brickyard, Let me throw 'em over the cliff for you, it'll save you one leg of the trip.

It's heavy work loading the barrow, he said.

Oh, well, said she.

All right, so long as you want to. But bricks are heavy bastards. Don't try to carry many. I'll give you the small barrow. And the little rat here can sit on the load and get a ride.

So she helped him on and off through days of silvery weather,

fog in the morning, clear sea and sky all afternoon, and the weeds in crannies of the cliff flowering; there was nothing else left to flower. The causeway ran out many yards from shore now, and Lif had had to learn a skill which no one else had ever learned that he knew of, except the fish. He could float and move himself about on the water or under it, in the very sea, without touching foot or hand to solid earth.

He had never heard that a man could do this thing; but he did not think much about it, being so busy with his bricks, in and out of air and in and out of water all day long, with the foam, the bubbles of water-circled air or air-circled water, all about him, and the fog, and the April rain, a confusion of the elements. Sometimes he was happy down in the murky green unbreathable world, wrestling strangely willful and weightless bricks among the staring shoals, and only the need of air drove him gasping up into the spray-laden wind.

He built all day long, scrambling up on the sand to collect the bricks that his faithful helper dumped over the cliff's edge for him, load them in his barrow and run them out the causeway that went straight out a foot or two under sea level at low tide and four or five feet under at high, then dump them at the end, dive in, and build; then back ashore for another load. He came up into town only at evening, worn out, salt-bleared and salt-itching, hungry as a shark, to share what food turned up with the widow and her little boy. Lately, though spring was getting on with soft, long, warm evenings, the town was very dark and still.

One night when he was not too tired to notice this he spoke of it, and the widow said, Oh, they're all gone now, I think.

—All! A pause. —Where did they go?

She shrugged. She raised her dark eyes to his across the table and gazed through lamplit silence at him for a time. Where? she said. Where does your sea-road lead, Lif?

He stayed still a while. To the Islands, he answered at last, and then laughed and met her look.

She did not laugh. She only said, Are they there? Is it true,

then, there are Islands? Then she looked over at her sleeping
baby, and out the open doorway into the darkness of late spring
that lay warm in the streets where no one walked and the rooms
where no one lived. At last she looked back at Lif, and said to
him, Lif, you know, there aren't many bricks left. A few hun-
dred. You'll have to make some more. Then she began to cry
softly.

By God! said Lif, thinking of his underwater road across the
sea that went for a hundred and twenty feet, and the sea that
went on ten thousand miles from the end of it— I'll swim there!
Now then, don't cry, dear heart. Would I leave you and the
little rat here by yourselves? After all the bricks you've nearly
hit my head with, and all the queer weeds and shellfish you've
found us to eat lately, after your table and fireside and your bed
and your laughter would I leave you when you cry? Now be
still, don't cry. Let me think of a way we can get to the Islands,
all of us together.

But he knew there was no way. Not for a brickmaker. He had
done what he could do. What he could do went one hundred
and twenty feet from shore.

Do you think, he asked after a long time, during which she
had cleared the table and rinsed the plates in wellwater that
was coming clear again now that the Ragers had been gone
many days— Do you think that maybe . . . this . . . He found it
hard to say but she stood quiet, waiting, and he had to say it:
That this *is* the end?

Stillness. In the one lamplit room and all the dark rooms and
streets and the burnt fields and wasted lands, stillness. In the
black Hall above them on the hill's height, stillness. A silent air,
a silent sky, silence in all places unbroken, unreplying. Except
for the far sound of the sea, and, very soft though nearer, the
breathing of a sleeping child.

No, the woman said. She sat down across from him and put
her hands upon the table, fine hands as dark as earth, the palms
like ivory. No, she said, the end will be the end. This is still just
the waiting for it.

Then why are we still here – just us?

Oh, well, she said, you had your things – your bricks – and I had the baby . . .

Tomorrow we must go, he said after a time. She nodded.

Before sunrise they were up. There was nothing at all left to eat, and so when she had put a few clothes for the baby in a bag and had on her warm leather mantle, and he had stuck his knife and trowel in his belt and put on a warm cloak that had been her husband's, they left the little house, going out into the cold wan light in the deserted streets.

They went downhill, he leading, she following with the sleepy child in a fold of her cloak. He turned neither to the road that led north up the coast nor to the southern road, but went on past the market place and out on the cliff and down the rocky path to the beach. All the way she followed and neither of them spoke. At the edge of the sea he turned.

I'll keep you up in the water as long as we can manage, he said.

She nodded, and said softly, We'll use the road you built, as far as it goes.

He took her free hand and led her into the water. It was cold. It was bitter cold, and the cold light from the east behind them shone on the foam-lines hissing on the sand. When they stepped on the beginning of the causeway the bricks were firm under their feet, and the child had gone back to sleep on her shoulder in a fold of her cloak.

As they went on the buffeting of the waves got stronger. The tide was coming in. The outer breakers wet their clothes, chilled their flesh, drenched their hair and faces. They reached the end of his long work. There lay the beach a little way behind them, the sand dark under the cliff over which stood the silent, paling sky. Around them was wild water and foam. Ahead of them was the unresting water, the great abyss, the gap.

A breaker hit them on its way in to shore and they staggered; the baby, waked by the sea's hard slap, cried, a little wail in the

long, cold, hissing mutter of the sea always saying the same thing.

Oh, I can't! cried the mother, but she gripped the man's hand more firmly and came on at his side.

Lifting his head to take the last step from what he had done towards no shore, he saw the shape riding the western water, the leaping light, the white flicker like a swallow's breast catching the break of day. It seemed as if voices rang over the sea's voice. What is it? he said, but her head was bowed to her baby, trying to soothe the little wail that challenged the vast babbling of the sea. He stood still and saw the whiteness of the sail, the dancing light above the waves, dancing on towards them and towards the greater light that grew behind them.

Wait, the call came from the form that rode the grey waves and danced on the foam, Wait! The voices rang very sweet, and as the sail leaned white above him he saw the faces and the reaching arms, and heard them say to him, Come, come on the ship, come with us to the Islands.

Hold on, he said softly to the woman, and they took the last step.

A TRIP TO THE HEAD

Most people 'lead lives of quiet desperation', and some stories
start there, too. We were in England and it was November and
dark at two in the afternoon and raining and the suitcase con-
taining all my manuscripts had been stolen at the dock in
Southampton and I hadn't written anything for months and I
couldn't understand the greengrocer and he couldn't under-
stand me and it was desperation – but quiet – stiff upper lip,
don't you know. So I sat down and started scribbling words,
perfectly hopelessly. Words, words, words. They went on about
as far as ' "Try being Amanda", the other said sourly,' and
stopped. A year or so later (British Rail, all honor to them, had
found my stolen suitcase, we were back home in Oregon, it was
raining) I found the scribble, and went on scribbling, and came
to the end. I never did find out what the title ought to be – my
agent, Virginia Kidd, did that, to my delight.

There is a kind of story which I would describe as a Bung
Puller. The writer for one reason or another has been stuck,
can't work; and gets started again suddenly, with a pop, and a
lot of beer comes leaping out of the keg and foaming all over the
floor. This story was definitely a Bung Puller.

'Is this Earth?' he cried, for things had changed abruptly.

'Yes, this is Earth,' said the one beside him, 'nor are you out
of it. In Zambia men are rolling down hills inside barrels as
training for space flight. Israel and Egypt have defoliated each
other's deserts. The *Reader's Digest* has bought a controlling
interest in the United States of America/General Mills com-
bine. The population of the Earth is increasing by thirty billion

18

every Thursday. Mrs Jacqueline Kennedy Onassis will marry Mao Tse-Tung on Saturday, in search of security; and Russia has contaminated Mars with bread mold.'

'Why then,' said he, 'nothing has changed.'

'Nothing much,' said the one beside him. 'As Jean-Paul Sartre has said in his lovable way, "Hell is other people." '

'To Hell with Jean-Paul Sartre. I want to know where I am.'

'Well then,' said the other, 'tell me who you are.'

'I'm.'

'Well?'

'My name is.'

'What?'

He stood, his eyes filling with tears and his knees with palsy, and knew he did not know his name. He was a blank, a cipher, an x. He had a body and all that, but he had no who.

They stood at the edge of a forest, he and the other one. It was a recognizable forest, though rather dingy in the leaf, and damaged at the fringes by weedkiller. A fawn was walking away from them into the forest and as it went its name fell away from it. Something looked back at them with mild eyes from the darkness of the trees before it vanished. 'This is England!' cried blank, grasping the floating straw, but the other said, 'England sank years ago.'

'Sank?'

'Yes. Foundered. Nothing is left now but the topmost fourteen feet of Mt Snowdon, known as the New Welsh Reef.'

At this blank also sank. He was crushed. 'Oh,' he cried on his knees, intending to ask somebody's help, but he could not remember whose help it was one asked. It began with a T, he was almost certain. He began to weep.

The other sat down on the grass beside him and presently put a hand on his shoulder, saying, 'Come one now, don't take it so hard.'

The kindly voice gave blank some courage. He controlled himself, dried his face on his sleeve, and looked at the other. It

was like him, roughly. It was another. However, it had no name either. What good was it?

Shadow came into the eyes as Earth went round on its axis. Shadow slipped eastward and upward into the other's eyes.

'I think,' blank said carefully, 'that we should move out from the shadow of the, this, here.' He gestured to the objects near them, large things, dark below and multitudinously green above, the names of which he could no longer remember. He wondered if each one had a name, or if they were all called by the same name. What about himself and the other, did they share a name in common, or did each have one of his own? 'I have a feeling I'll remember better farther away from it, from them,' he said.

'Certainly,' said the other. 'But it won't make as much difference as it used to.'

When they came clear away from it into the sunlight, he at once remembered that it was called a forest and that they were called trees. However, he could not recall whether or not each tree had a name of its own. If they did, he did not remember any of them. Perhaps he did not know these trees personally.

'What shall I do,' he said, 'what shall I do?'

'Well, look here, you can call yourself whatever you please, you know. Why not?'

'But I want to know my *real* name.'

'That isn't always easy. But meanwhile you could just take a label, as it were, for ease of reference and conversational purposes. Pick a name, any name!' said the other, and held out a blue box named DISPOSABLE.

'No,' said Blank proudly, 'I'll choose my own.'

'Right. But don't you want a kleenex?'

Blank took a kleenex, blew his nose, and said, 'I shall call myself . . .' He halted in terror.

The other watched him, mild-eyed.

'How can I say who I am when I can't say what I am?'

'How would you find out what you are?'

'If I had anything— If I did something—'

'That would make you be?'

'Of course it would.'

'I never thought of that. Well, then, it doesn't matter what name you're called by; any one will do; it's what you do that counts.'

Blank stood up. 'I will exist,' he stated firmly. 'I will call myself Ralph.'

Whipcord breeches fitted close on his powerful thighs, the stock rose high on his neck, sweat clung in his thick, curly hair. He tapped his boots with his riding-crop, his back to Amanda, who sat in her old grey dress in the deep shade of the pecan tree. He stood in full sunlight, hot with anger. 'You're a fool,' he said.

'Why Mr Ralph,' came the soft lilting Southern voice, 'Ah'm just a little bit stubborn.'

'You realize, don't you, that Yankee as I am, I own all the land from here to Weevilville? I own this county! Your farm wouldn't make a peanut-patch for one of my darkies' kitchen gardens!'

'Indeed not. Won't you come sit down in the shade, Mr Ralph? Youah gettin' so hot out theah.'

'You proud vixen,' he murmured, turning. He saw her, white as a lily in her worn old dress, in the shade of the great old trees: the white lily of the garden. Suddenly he was at her feet, clasping her hands. She fluttered in his powerful grasp. 'Oh Mr Ralph,' she cried faintly, 'what does this mean?'

'I am a man, Amanda, and you are a woman. I never wanted your land. I never wanted anything but you, my white lily, my little rebel! I want you, I want you! Amanda! Say you will be my wife!'

'Ah will,' she breathed faintly, bending towards him as a white flower stoops; and their lips met in a long, long kiss. But it did not seem to help at all.

Perhaps it ought to be moved up twenty or thirty years.

'You sick bitch,' he muttered, turning. He saw her, stark naked there in the shade, her back against the pecan tree, her

knees up. He strode towards her unbuttoning his fly. They coupled in the centipede-infested crabgrass. He bucked like a bronco, she cried ululatingly, *Oooh! Aaah!* Coming coming coming COME WOW WOW WOW CLIMAX!

Now what?

Blank stood at a little distance from the forest and stared disconsolately at the other.

'Am I a man?' he inquired. 'Are you a woman?'

'Don't ask me,' the other said, morose.

'I thought surely that was the most important thing to establish!'

'Not so damned important.'

'You mean it doesn't *matter* if I am a man or a woman?'

'Of course it matters. It matters to me too. It also matters which man and which woman we are or, as the case may be, are not. For instance, what if Amanda was black?'

'But sex.'

'Oh, Hell,' said the other with a flare of temper, 'bristle-worms have sex, tree-sloths have sex, Jean-Paul Sartre has sex – what does it prove?'

'Why, sex is real, I mean really real – it's having and acting in its intensest form. When a man takes a woman he proves his being!'

'I see. But what if he's a woman?'

'I was Ralph.'

'Try being Amanda,' the other said sourly.

There was a pause. Shadows were coming on eastward and upward from the forest over the grass. Small birds cried *jug jug, tereu*. Blank sat hunched over his knees. The other lay stretched out, making patterns with fallen pine needles, shadowed, sorrowful.

'I'm sorry,' blank said.

'No harm done,' the other said. 'After all, it wasn't real.'

'Listen,' blank said, leaping up, 'I know what's happened! I'm on some kind of trip. I took something, and I'm on a trip, that's it!'

It was. He was on a trip. A canoe trip. He was paddling a small canoe along a long, narrow, dark, shining stretch of water. The roof and walls were of concrete. It was pretty dark. The long lake, or stream, or sewer, slanted upward visibly. He was paddling against the current, uphill. It was hard work, but the canoe kept sliding forward upriver as silently as the black shining water moved back down. He kept his strokes quiet, the paddle entering the water silent as a knife in butter. His large black-and-pearl electric guitar lay on the forward seat. He knew there was somebody behind him, but he didn't say anything. He wasn't allowed to say anything or even look around, so if they didn't keep up that was their lookout, he couldn't be called responsible. He certainly couldn't slow down, the current might get hold of his canoe and pull it right out from under him and then where'd he be? He shut his eyes and kept paddling, silent entry, strong stroke. There was no sound behind him. The water made no sound. The cement made no sound. He wondered if he was actually going forward or only hanging still while the black water ran hellbent beneath. He would never get out to daylight. Out, out—

The other didn't even seem to have noticed that blank had been away on a trip, but just lay there making patterns with pine needles, and presently said, 'How is your memory?'

Blank searched it to see if it had improved while he was away. There was less in it than before. The cupboard was bare. There was a lot of junk in the cellars and attics, old toys, nursery rhymes, myths, old wives' tales, but no nourishment for adults, no least scrap of possession, not a crumb of success. He searched and searched like a starving methodical rat. At last he said uncertainly, 'I do remember England.'

'Why surely. I expect you can even remember Omaha.'

'But I mean, I remember being in England.'

'Do you?' The other sat up, scattering pinestraw. 'You do remember being, then! What a pity England sank.'

They were silent again.

'I have lost everything.'

There was a darkness in the other's eyes and on the eastern edge of the earth plunging down the steepening slopes of night.

'I'm nobody.'

'At least,' said the other, 'you know you're human.'

'Oh, what good's that? with no name, no sex, no nothing? I might as well be a bristleworm or a tree-sloth!'

'You might as well,' the other agreed, 'be Jean-Paul Sartre.'

'I?' said blank, offended. Driven to denial by so nauseous a notion, he stood up and said, 'I certainly am not Jean-Paul Sartre. I am myself.' And so saying he found himself to be, in fact, himself; his name was Lewis D. Charles and he knew it as well as he knew his own name. There he was.

The forest was there, root and branch.

The other was, however, gone.

Lewis D. Charles looked in the red eye of the west and the dark eye of the east. He shouted aloud, 'Come back! Please come back!'

He had gone at it all wrong, backwards. He had found the wrong name. He turned, and without the least impulse of self-preservation plunged into the pathless forest, casting himself away so that he might find what he had cast away.

Under the trees he forgot his name again at once. He also forgot what he was looking for. What was it he had lost? He went deeper and deeper into shadows, under leaves, eastward, in the forest where nameless tigers burned.

VASTER THAN EMPIRES AND MORE SLOW

Trees again.

As I recall, Robert Silverberg, who first published this story in New Dimensions 1, *asked very gently if I would change the title. I could see where a reader about halfway through might find the title all too descriptive of the story itself; but it was too beautiful, and too beautifully apt, to part with, and Mr Silverberg let me keep it. It's from Marvell, 'To his Coy Mistress'—*

> *Our vegetable love should grow*
> *Vaster than empires, and more slow . . .*

Like 'Nine Lives,' this is not a psychomyth but a regular science fiction story, developed not for action/adventure, but psychologically. Unless physical action reflects psychic action, unless the deeds express the person, I get very bored with adventure stories; often it seems that the more action there is, the less happens. Obviously my interest is in what goes on inside. Inner space and all that. We all have forests in our minds. Forests unexplored, unending. Each of us gets lost in the forest, every night, alone.

Hidden in the foliage here is a tiny act of homage. The protagonist of 'He Who Shapes' by Roger Zelazny, one of the finest science fiction stories I know, is called Charles Render. I christened a syndrome after him.

It was only during the earliest decades of the League that the Earth sent ships out on the enormously long voyages, beyond the pale, over the stars and far away. They were seeking for

worlds which had not been seeded or settled by the Founders on Hain, truly alien worlds. All the Known Worlds went back to the Hainish Origin, and the Terrans, having been not only founded but salvaged by the Hainish, resented this. They wanted to get away from the family. They wanted to find somebody new. The Hainish, like tiresomely understanding parents, supported their explorations, and contributed ships and volunteers, as did several other worlds of the League.

All these volunteers to the Extreme Survey crews shared one peculiarity: they were of unsound mind.

What sane person, after all, would go out to collect information that would not be received for five or ten centuries? Cosmic mass interference had not yet been eliminated from the operation of the ansible, and so instantaneous communication was reliable only within a range of 120 lightyears. The explorers would be quite isolated. And of course they had no idea what they might come back to, if they came back. No normal human being who had experienced time-slippage of even a few decades between League worlds would volunteer for a round trip of centuries. The Surveyors were escapists, misfits. They were nuts.

Ten of them climbed aboard the ferry at Smeming Port, and made varyingly inept attempts to get to know one another during the three days the ferry took getting to their ship, *Gum*. Gum is a Cetian nickname, on the order of Baby or Pet. There were two Cetians on the team, two Hainishmen, one Beldene, and five Terrans; the Cetian-built ship was chartered by the Government of Earth. Her motley crew came aboard wriggling through the coupling tube one by one like apprehensive spermatozoa trying to fertilize the universe. The ferry left, and the navigator put *Gum* underway. She flittered for some hours on the edge of space a few hundred million miles from Smeming Port, and then abruptly vanished.

When, after 10 hours 29 minutes, or 256 years, *Gum* reappeared in normal space, she was supposed to be in the vicinity of Star KG–E–96651. Sure enough, there was the gold

pinhead of the star. Somewhere within a four-hundred-million-kilometer sphere there was also a greenish planet, World 4470, as charted by a Cetian mapmaker. The ship now had to find the planet. This was not quite so easy as it might sound, given a four-hundred-million-kilometer haystack. And *Gum* couldn't bat about in planetary space at near lightspeed; if she did, she and Star KG–E–96651 and World 4470 might all end up going bang. She had to creep, using rocket propulsion, at a few hundred thousand miles an hour. The Mathematician/Navigator, Asnanifoil, knew pretty well where the planet ought to be, and thought they might raise it within ten E-days. Meanwhile the members of the Survey team got to know one another still better.

'I can't stand him,' said Porlock, the Hard Scientist (chemistry, plus physics, astronomy, geology, etc.), and little blobs of spittle appeared on his mustache. 'The man is insane. I can't imagine why he was passed as fit to join a Survey team, unless this is a deliberate experiment in noncompatibility, planned by the Authority, with us as guinea pigs.'

'We generally use hamsters and Hainish gholes,' said Mannon, the Soft Scientist (psychology, plus psychiatry, anthropology, ecology, etc.), politely; he was one of the Hainishmen. 'Instead of guinea pigs. Well, you know, Mr Osden is really a very rare case. In fact, he's the first fully cured case of Render's Syndrome – a variety of infantile autism which was thought to be incurable. The great Terran analyst Hammergeld reasoned that the cause of the autistic condition in this case is a supernormal empathic capacity, and developed an appropriate treatment. Mr Osden is the first patient to undergo that treatment, in fact he lived with Dr Hammergeld until he was eighteen. The therapy was completely successful.'

'Successful?'

'Why, yes. He certainly is not autistic.'

'No, he's intolerable!'

'Well, you see,' said Mannon, gazing mildly at the saliva-flecks on Porlock's mustache, 'the normal defensive-aggressive

reaction between strangers meeting – let's say you and Mr Osden just for example – is something you're scarcely aware of; habit, manners, inattention get you past it; you've learned to ignore it, to the point where you might even deny it exists. However, Mr Osden, being an empath, feels it. Feels his feelings, and yours, and is hard put to say which is which. Let's say that there's a normal element of hostility towards any stranger in your emotional reaction to him when you meet him, plus a spontaneous dislike of his looks, or clothes, or handshake – it doesn't matter what. He feels that dislike. As his autistic defense has been unlearned, he resorts to an aggressive-defense mechanism, a response in kind to the aggression which you have unwittingly projected onto him.' Mannon went on for quite a long time.

'Nothing gives a man the right to be such a bastard,' Porlock said.

'He can't tune us out?' asked Harfex, the Biologist, another Hainishman.

'It's like hearing,' said Olleroo, Assistant Hard Scientist, stooping over to paint her toenails with fluorescent lacquer. 'No eyelids on your ears. No Off switch on empathy. He hears our feelings whether he wants to or not.'

'Does he know what we're *thinking*?' asked Eskwana, the Engineer, looking round at the others in real dread.

'No,' Porlock snapped. 'Empathy's not telepathy! Nobody's got telepathy.'

'Yet,' said Mannon, with his little smile. 'Just before I left Hain there was a most interesting report in from one of the recently rediscovered worlds, a hilfer named Rocannon reporting what appears to be a teachable telepathic technique existent among a mutated hominid race; I only saw a synopsis in the HILF Bulletin, but—' He went on. The others had learned that they could talk while Mannon went on talking; he did not seem to mind, nor even to miss much of what they said.

'Then why does he hate us?' Eskwana said.

'Nobody hates you, Ander honey,' said Olleroo, daubing Es-

kwana's left thumbnail with fluorescent pink. The engineer flushed and smiled vaguely.

'He acts as if he hated us,' said Haito, the Coordinator. She was a delicate-looking woman of pure Asian descent, with a surprising voice, husky, deep, and soft, like a young bullfrog. 'Why, if he suffers from our hostility, does he increase it by constant attacks and insults? I can't say I think much of Dr Hammergeld's cure, really, Mannon; autism might be preferable . . .'

She stopped. Osden had come into the main cabin.

He looked flayed. His skin was unnaturally white and thin, showing the channels of his blood like a faded road map in red and blue. His Adam's apple, the muscles that circled his mouth, the bones and ligaments of his wrists and hands, all stood out distinctly as if displayed for an anatomy lesson. His hair was pale rust, like long-dried blood. He had eyebrows and lashes, but they were visible only in certain lights; what one saw was the bones of the eye sockets, the veining of the lids, and the colorless eyes. They were not red eyes, for he was not really an albino, but they were not blue or grey; colors had cancelled out in Osden's eyes, leaving a cold water-like clarity, infinitely penetrable. He never looked directly at one. His face lacked expression, like an anatomical drawing, or a skinned face.

'I agree,' he said in a high, harsh tenor, 'that even autistic withdrawal might be preferable to the smog of cheap secondhand emotions with which you people surround me. What are you sweating hate for now, Porlock? Can't stand the sight of me? Go practice some auto-eroticism the way you were doing last night, it improves your vibes. Who the devil moved my tapes, here? Don't touch my things, any of you. I won't have it.'

'Osden,' said Asnanifoil in his large slow voice, 'why *are* you such a bastard?'

Ander Eskwana cowered and put his hands in front of his face. Contention frightened him. Olleroo looked up with a vacant yet eager expression, the eternal spectator.

'Why shouldn't I be?' said Osden. He was not looking at

Asnanifoil, and was keeping physically as far away from all of them as he could in the crowded cabin. 'None of you constitute, in yourselves, any reason for my changing my behavior.'

Harfex, a reserved and patient man, said, 'The reason is that we shall be spending several years together. Life will be better for all of us if—'

'Can't you understand that I don't give a damn for all of you?' Osden said, took up his microtapes, and went out. Eskwana had suddenly gone to sleep. Asnanifoil was drawing slip-streams in the air with his finger and muttering the Ritual Primes. 'You cannot explain his presence on the team except as a plot on the part of the Terran Authority. I saw this almost at once. This mission is meant to fail,' Harfex whispered to the Coordinator, glancing over his shoulder. Porlock was fumbling with his fly-button; there were tears in his eyes. 'I did tell you they were all crazy, but you thought I was exaggerating.'

All the same, they were not unjustified. Extreme Surveyors expected to find their fellow team members intelligent, well-trained, unstable, and personally sympathetic. They had to work together in close quarters and nasty places, and could expect one another's paranoias, depressions, manias, phobias and compulsions to be mild enough to admit of good personal relationships, at least most of the time. Osden might be intelligent, but his training was sketchy and his personality was disastrous. He had been sent only on account of his singular gift, the power of empathy: properly speaking, of wide-range bio-empathic receptivity. His talent wasn't species-specific; he could pick up emotion or sentience from anything that felt. He could share lust with a white rat, pain with a squashed cockroach, and phototropy with a moth. On an alien world, the Authority had decided, it would be useful to know if anything nearby is sentient, and if so, what its feelings towards you are. Osden's title was a new one: he was the team's Sensor.

'What is emotion, Osden?' Haito Tomiko asked him one day in the main cabin, trying to make some rapport with him for

once. 'What is it, exactly, that you pick up with your empathic sensitivity?'

'Muck,' the man answered in his high, exasperated voice. 'The psychic excreta of the animal kingdom. I wade through your faeces.'

'I was trying,' she said, 'to learn some facts.' She thought her tone was admirably calm.

'You weren't after facts. You were trying to get at me. With some fear, some curiosity, and a great deal of distaste. The way you might poke a dead dog, to see the maggots crawl. Will you understand once and for all that I don't want to be got at, that I want to be left alone?' His skin was mottled with red and violet, his voice had risen. 'Go roll in your own dung, you yellow bitch!' he shouted at her silence.

'Calm down,' she said, still quietly, but she left him at once and went to her cabin. Of course he had been right about her motives; her question had been largely a pretext, a mere effort to interest him. But what harm in that? Did not that effort imply respect for the other? At the moment of asking the question she had felt at most a slight distrust of him; she had mostly felt sorry for him, the poor arrogant venomous bastard, Mr No-skin as Olleroo called him. What did he expect, the way he acted? Love?

'I guess he can't stand anybody feeling sorry for him,' said Olleroo, lying on the lower bunk, gilding her nipples.

'Then he can't form any human relationship. All his Dr Hammergeld did was turn an autism inside out. . . .'

'Poor frot,' said Olleroo. 'Tomiko, you don't mind if Harfex comes in for a while tonight, do you?'

'Can't you go to his cabin? I'm sick of always having to sit in Main with that damned peeled turnip.'

'You do hate him, don't you? I guess he feels that. But I slept with Harfex last night too, and Asnanifoil might get jealous, since they share the cabin. It would be nicer here.'

'Service them both,' Tomiko said with the coarseness of

offended modesty. Her Terran subculture, the East Asian, was a puritanical one; she had been brought up chaste.

'I only like one a night,' Olleroo replied with innocent serenity. Beldene, the Garden Planet, had never discovered chastity, or the wheel.

'Try Osden, then,' Tomiko said. Her personal instability was seldom so plain as now: a profound self-distrust manifesting itself as destructivism. She had volunteered for this job because there was, in all probability, no use in doing it.

The little Beldene looked up, paintbrush in hand, eyes wide. 'Tomiko, that was a dirty thing to say.'

'Why?'

'It would be vile! I'm not attracted to Osden!'

'I didn't know it mattered to you,' Tomiko said indifferently, though she did know. She got some papers together and left the cabin, remarking, 'I hope you and Harfex or whoever it is finish by last bell; I'm tired.'

Olleroo was crying, tears dripping on her little gilded nipples. She wept easily. Tomiko had not wept since she was ten years old.

It was not a happy ship; but it took a turn for the better when Asnanifoil and his computers raised World 4470. There it lay, a dark-green jewel, like truth at the bottom of a gravity well. As they watched the jade disc grow, a sense of mutuality grew among them. Osden's selfishness, his accurate cruelty, served now to draw the others together. 'Perhaps,' Mannon said, 'he was sent as a beating-gron. What Terrans call a scapegoat. Perhaps his influence will be good after all.' And no one, so careful were they to be kind to one another, disagreed.

They came into orbit. There were no lights on nightside, on the continents none of the lines and clots made by animals who build.

'No men,' Harfex murmured.

'Of course not,' snapped Osden, who had a viewscreen to himself, and his head inside a polythene bag. He claimed that the plastic cut down on the empathic noise he received from the others. 'We're two lightcenturies past the limit of the Hainish

Expansion, and outside that there are no men. Anywhere. You don't think Creation would have made the same hideous mistake twice?'

No one was paying him much heed; they were looking with affection at that jade immensity below them, where there was life, but not human life. They were misfits among men, and what they saw there was not desolation, but peace. Even Osden did not look quite so expressionless as usual; he was frowning.

Descent in fire on the sea; air reconnaissance; landing. A plain of something like grass, thick, green, bowing stalks, surrounded the ship, brushed against extended viewcameras, smeared the lenses with a fine pollen.

'It looks like a pure phytosphere,' Harfex said. 'Osden, do you pick up anything sentient?'

They all turned to the Sensor. He had left the screen and was pouring himself a cup of tea. He did not answer. He seldom answered spoken questions.

The chitinous rigidity of military discipline was quite inapplicable to these teams of mad scientists; their chain of command lay somewhere between parliamentary procedure and peck-order, and would have driven a regular service officer out of his mind. By the inscrutable decision of the Authority, however, Dr Haito Tomiko had been given the title of Coordinator, and she now exercised her prerogative for the first time. 'Mr Sensor Osden,' she said, 'please answer Mr Harfex.'

'How could I "pick up" anything from outside,' Osden said without turning, 'with the emotions of nine neurotic hominids pullulating around me like worms in a can? When I have anything to tell you, I'll tell you. I'm aware of my responsibility as Sensor. If you presume to give me an order again, however, Coordinator Haito, I'll consider my responsibility void.'

'Very well, Mr Sensor. I trust no orders will be needed henceforth.' Tomiko's bullfrog voice was calm, but Osden seemed to flinch slightly as he stood with his back to her, as if the surge of her suppressed rancor had struck him with physical force.

T—B

The biologist's hunch proved correct. When they began field analyses they found no animals even among the microbiota. Nobody here ate anybody else. All life-forms were photo-synthesizing or saprophagous, living off light or death, not off life. Plants: infinite plants, not one species known to the visitors from the house of Man. Infinite shades and intensities of green, violet, purple, brown, red. Infinite silences. Only the wind moved, swaying leaves and fronds, a warm soughing wind laden with spores and pollens, blowing the sweet pale-green dust over prairies of great grasses, heaths that bore no heather, flowerless forests where no foot had ever walked, no eye had ever looked. A warm, sad world, sad and serene. The Surveyors, wandering like picnickers over sunny plains of violet filicaliformes, spoke softly to each other. They knew their voices broke a silence of a thousand million years, the silence of wind and leaves, leaves and wind, blowing and ceasing and blowing again. They talked softly; but being human, they talked.

'Poor old Osden,' said Jenny Chong, Bio and Tech, as she piloted a helijet on the North Polar Quadrating run. 'All that fancy hi-fi stuff in his brain and nothing to receive. What a bust.'

'He told me he hates plants,' Olleroo said with a giggle.

'You'd think he'd like them, since they don't bother him like we do.'

'Can't say I much like these plants myself,' said Porlock, looking down at the purple undulations of the North Circumpolar Forest. 'All the same. No mind. No change. A man alone in it would go right off his head,'

'But it's all alive,' Jenny Chong said. 'And if it lives, Osden hates it.'

'He's not really so bad,' Olleroo said, magnanimous. Porlock looked at her sidelong and asked, 'You ever slept with him, Olleroo?'

Olleroo burst into tears and cried, 'You Terrans are obscene!'

'No she hasn't,' Jenny Chong said, prompt to defend. 'Have you, Porlock?'

The chemist laughed uneasily: ha, ha, ha. Flecks of spittle appeared on his mustache.

'Osden can't bear to be touched,' Olleroo said shakily. 'I just brushed against him once by accident and he knocked me off like I was some sort of dirty . . . thing. We're all just things, to him.'

'He's evil,' Porlock said in a strained voice, startling the two women. 'He'll end up shattering this team, sabotaging it, one way or another. Mark my words. He's not fit to live with other people!'

They landed on the North Pole. A midnight sun smouldered over low hills. Short, dry, greenish-pink bryoform grasses stretched away in every direction, which was all one direction, south. Subdued by the incredible silence, the three Surveyors set up their instruments and set to work, three viruses twitching minutely on the hide of an unmoving giant.

Nobody asked Osden along on runs as pilot or photographer or recorder, and he never volunteered, so he seldom left base camp. He ran Harfex's botanical taxonomic data through the onship computers, and served as assistant to Eskwana, whose job here was mainly repair and maintenance. Eskwana had begun to sleep a great deal, twenty-five hours or more out of the thirty-two-hour day, dropping off in the middle of repairing a radio or checking the guidance circuits of a helijet. The Coordinator stayed at base one day to observe. No one else was home except Poswet To, who was subject to epileptic fits; Mannon had plugged her into a therapy-circuit today in a state of preventive catatonia. Tomiko spoke reports into the storage banks, and kept an eye on Osden and Eskwana. Two hours passed.

'You might want to use the 860 microwaldoes in sealing that connection,' Eskwana said in his soft, hesitant voice.

'Obviously!'

'Sorry. I just saw you had the 840's there—'

'And will replace them when I take the 860's out. When

I don't know how to proceed, Engineer, I'll ask your advice.'

After a minute Tomiko looked round. Sure enough, there was Eskwana sound asleep, head on the table, thumb in his mouth.

'Osden.'

The white face did not turn, he did not speak, but conveyed impatiently that he was listening.

'You can't be unaware of Eskwana's vulnerability.'

'I am not responsible for his psychopathic reactions.'

'But you are responsible for your own. Eskwana is essential to our work here, and you're not. If you can't control your hostility, you must avoid him altogether.'

Osden put down his tools and stood up. 'With pleasure!' he said in his vindictive, scraping voice. 'You could not possibly imagine what it's like to experience Eskwana's irrational terrors. To have to share his horrible cowardice, to have to cringe with him at everything!'

'Are you trying to justify your cruelty towards him? I thought you had more self-respect.' Tomiko found herself shaking with spite. 'If your empathic power really makes you share Ander's misery, why does it never induce the least compassion in you?'

'Compassion,' Osden said. 'Compassion. What do you know about compassion?'

She stared at him, but he would not look at her.

'Would you like me to verbalize your present emotional affect regarding myself?' he said. 'I can do so more precisely than you can. I'm trained to analyze such responses as I receive them. And I do receive them.'

'But how can you expect me to feel kindly towards you when you behave as you do?'

'What does it matter how I *behave*, you stupid sow, do you think it makes any difference? Do you think the average human is a well of loving-kindness? My choice is to be hated or to be despised. Not being a woman or a coward, I prefer to be hated.'

'That's rot. Self-pity. Every man has—'

'But I am not a man,' Osden said. 'There are all of you. And there is myself. I am *one*.'

Awed by that glimpse of abysmal solipsism, she kept silent a while; finally she said with neither spite nor pity, clinically, 'You could kill yourself, Osden.'

'That's your way, Haito,' he jeered. 'I'm not depressive, and *seppuku* isn't my bit. What do you want me to do here?'

'Leave. Spare yourself and us. Take the aircar and a data-feeder and go do a species count. In the forest; Harfex hasn't even started the forests yet. Take a hundred-square-meter forested area, anywhere inside radio range. But outside empathy range. Report in at 8 and 24 o'clock daily.'

Osden went, and nothing was heard from him for five days but laconic all-well signals twice daily. The mood at base camp changed like a stage-set. Eskwana stayed awake up to eighteen hours a day. Poswet To got out her stellar lute and chanted the celestial harmonies (music had driven Osden into a frenzy). Mannon, Harfex, Jenny Chong, and Tomiko all went off tranquillizers. Porlock distilled something in his laboratory and drank it all by himself. He had a hangover. Asnanifoil and Poswet To held an all-night Numerical Epiphany, that mystical orgy of higher mathematics which is the chief pleasure of the religious Cetian soul. Olleroo slept with everybody. Work went well.

The Hard Scientist came towards base at a run, laboring through the high, fleshy stalks of the graminiformes. 'Something – in the forest—' His eyes bulged, he panted, his mustache and fingers trembled. 'Something big. Moving, behind me. I was putting in a benchmark, bending down. It came at me. As if it was swinging down out of the trees. Behind me.' He stared at the others with the opaque eyes of terror or exhaustion.

'Sit down, Porlock. Take it easy. Now wait, go through this again. You *saw* something—'

'Not clearly. Just the movement. Purposive. A – an – I don't know what it could have been. Something self-moving. In the trees, the arboriformes, whatever you call 'em. At the edge of the woods.'

Harfex looked grim. 'There is nothing here that could attack you, Porlock. There are not even microzoa. There *could not* be a large animal.'

'Could you possibly have seen an epiphyte drop suddenly, a vine come loose behind you?'

'No', Porlock said. 'It was coming down at me, through the branches, fast. When I turned it took off again, away and upward. It made a noise, a sort of crashing. If it wasn't an animal, God knows what it could have been! It was big – as big as a man, at least. Maybe a reddish color. I couldn't see, I'm not sure.'

'It was Osden,' said Jenny Chong, 'doing a Tarzan act.' She giggled nervously, and Tomiko repressed a wild feckless laugh. But Harfex was not smiling.

'One gets uneasy under the arboriformes,' he said in his polite, repressed voice. 'I've noticed that. Indeed that may be why I've put off working in the forests. There's a hypnotic quality in the colors and spacing of the stems and branches, especially the helically-arranged ones; and the spore-throwers grow so regularly spaced that it seems unnatural. I find it quite disagreeable, subjectively speaking. I wonder if a stronger effect of that sort mightn't have produced a hallucination . . .?'

Porlock shook his head. He wet his lips. 'It was there,' he said. 'Something. Moving with purpose. Trying to attack me from behind.'

When Osden called in, punctual as always, at 24 o'clock that night, Harfex told him Porlock's report. 'Have you come on anything at all, Mr Osden, that could substantiate Mr Porlock's impression of a motile, sentient life-form, in the forest?'

Ssss, the radio said sardonically. 'No. Bullshit,' said Osden's unpleasant voice.

'You've been actually inside the forest longer than any of us,' Harfex said with unmitigable politeness. 'Do you agree with my impression that the forest ambiance has a rather troubling and possibly hallucinogenic effect on the perceptions?'

Ssss. 'I'll agree that Porlock's perceptions are easily troubled. Keep him in his lab, he'll do less harm. Anything else?'

'Not at present,' Harfex said, and Osden cut off.

Nobody could credit Porlock's story, and nobody could discredit it. He was positive that something, something big, had tried to attack him by surprise. It was hard to deny this, for they were on an alien world, and everyone who had entered the forest had felt a certain chill and foreboding under the 'trees.' ('Call them trees, certainly,' Harfex had said. 'They really are the same thing, only, of course, altogether different.') They agreed that they had felt uneasy, or had had the sense that something was watching them from behind.

'We've got to clear this up,' Porlock said, and he asked to be sent as a temporary Biologist's Aide, like Osden, into the forest to explore and observe. Olleroo and Jenny Chong volunteered if they could go as a pair. Harfex sent them all off into the forest near which they were encamped, a vast tract covering four-fifths of Continent D. He forbade side-arms. They were not to go outside a fifty-mile half-circle, which included Osden's current site. They all reported in twice daily, for three days. Porlock reported a glimpse of what seemed to be a large semi-erect shape moving through the trees across the river; Olleroo was sure she had heard something moving near the tent, the second night.

'There are no animals on this planet,' Harfex said, dogged.

Then Osden missed his morning call.

Tomiko waited less than an hour, then flew with Harfex to the area where Osden had reported himself the night before. But as the helijet hovered over the sea of purplish leaves, illimitable, impenetrable, she felt a panic despair. 'How can we find him in this?'

'He reported landing on the riverbank. Find the aircar; he'll be camped near it, and he can't have gone far from his camp. Species-counting is slow work. There's the river.'

'There's his car,' Tomiko said, catching the bright foreign glint among the vegetable colors and shadows. 'Here goes, then.'

She put the ship in hover and pitched out the ladder. She and Harfex descended. The sea of life closed over their heads.

As her feet touched the forest floor, she unsnapped the flap of her holster; then glancing at Harfex, who was unarmed, she left the gun untouched. But her hand kept coming back up to it. There was no sound at all, as soon as they were a few meters away from the slow, brown river, and the light was dim. Great boles stood well apart, almost regularly, almost alike; they were soft-skinned, some appearing smooth and others spongy, grey or greenish-brown or brown, twined with cable-like creepers and festooned with epiphytes, extending rigid, entangled armfuls of big, saucer-shaped, dark leaves that formed a roof-layer twenty to thirty meters thick. The ground underfoot was springy as a mattress, every inch of it knotted with roots and peppered with small, fleshy-leaved growths.

'Here's his tent,' Tomiko said, cowed at the sound of her voice in that huge community of the voiceless. In the tent was Osden's sleeping bag, a couple of books, a box of rations. We should be calling, shouting for him, she thought, but did not even suggest it; nor did Harfex. They circled out from the tent, careful to keep each other in sight through the thick-standing presences, the crowding gloom. She stumbled over Osden's body, not thirty meters from the tent, led to it by the whitish gleam of a dropped notebook. He lay face down between two huge-rooted trees. His head and hands were covered with blood, some dried, some still oozing red.

Harfex appeared beside her, his pale Hainish complexion quite green in the dusk. 'Dead?'

'No. He's been struck. Beaten. From behind.' Tomiko's fingers felt over the bloody skull and temples and nape. 'A weapon or a tool . . . I don't find a fracture.'

As she turned Osden's body over so they could lift him, his eyes opened. She was holding him, bending close to his face.

His pale lips writhed. A deathly fear came into her. She screamed aloud two or three times and tried to run away, shambling and stumbling into the terrible dusk. Harfex caught her, and at his touch and the sound of his voice, her panic decreased. 'What is it? What is it?' he was saying.

'I don't know,' she sobbed. Her heartbeat still shook her, and she could not see clearly. 'The fear – the . . . I panicked. When I saw his eyes.'

'We're both nervous. I don't understand this—'

'I'm all right now, come on, we've got to get him under care.'

Both working with senseless haste, they lugged Osden to the riverside and hauled him up on a rope under his armpits; he dangled like a sack, twisting a little over the glutinous dark sea of leaves. They pulled him into the helijet and took off. Within a minute they were over open prairie. Tomiko locked onto the homing beam. She drew a deep breath, and her eyes met Harfex's.

'I was so terrified I almost fainted. I have never done that.'

'I was . . . unreasonably frightened also,' said the Hainish-man, and indeed he looked aged and shaken. 'Not so badly as you. But as unreasonably.'

'It was when I was in contact with him, holding him. He seemed to be conscious for a moment.'

'Empathy? . . . I hope he can tell us what attacked him.'

Osden, like a broken dummy covered with blood and mud, half lay as they had bundled him into the rear seats in their frantic urgency to get out of the forest.

More panic met their arrival at base. The ineffective brut-ality of the assault was sinister and bewildering. Since Harfex stubbornly denied any possibility of animal life they began speculating about sentient plants, vegetable monsters, psychic projections. Jenny Chong's latent phobia reasserted itself and she could talk about nothing except the Dark Egos which fol-lowed people around behind their backs. She and Olleroo and Porlock had been summoned back to base; and nobody was much inclined to go outside.

Osden had lost a good deal of blood during the three or four hours he had lain alone, and concussion and severe contusions had put him in shock and semi-coma. As he came out of this and began running a low fever he called several times for 'Doctor', in a plaintive voice: 'Doctor Hammergeld . . .' When he regained full consciousness, two of those long days later, Tomiko called Harfex into his cubicle.

'Osden: can you tell us what attacked you?'

The pale eyes flickered past Harfex's face.

'You were attacked,' Tomiko said gently. The shifty gaze was hatefully familiar, but she was a physician, protective of the hurt. 'You may not remember it yet. Something attacked you. You were in the forest—'

'Ah!' he cried out, his eyes growing bright and his features contorting. 'The forest – in the forest—'

'What's in the forest?'

He gasped for breath. A look of clearer consciousness came into his face. After a while he said, 'I don't know.'

'Did you see what attacked you?' Harfex asked.

'I don't know.'

'You remember it now.'

'I don't know.'

'All our lives may depend on this. You must tell us what you saw!'

'I don't know,' Osden said, sobbing with weakness. He was too weak to hide the fact that he was hiding the answer, yet he would not say it. Porlock, nearby, was chewing his pepper-colored mustache as he tried to hear what was going on in the cubicle. Harfex leaned over Osden and said, 'You *will* tell us—' Tomiko had to interfere bodily.

Harfex controlled himself with an effort that was painful to see. He went off silently to his cubicle, where no doubt he took a double or triple dose of tranquillizers. The other men and women, scattered about the big frail building, a long main hall and ten sleeping-cubicles, said nothing, but looked depressed and

edgy. Osden, as always, even now, had them all at his mercy. Tomiko looked down at him with a rush of hatred that burned in her throat like bile. This monstrous egotism that fed itself on others' emotion, this absolute selfishness, was worse than any hideous deformity of the flesh. Like a congenital monster, he should not have lived. Should not be alive. Should have died. Why had his head not been split open?

As he lay flat and white, his hands helpless at his sides, his colorless eyes were wide open, and there were tears running from the corners. He tried to flinch away. 'Don't,' he said in a weak hoarse voice, and tried to raise his hands to protect his head. 'Don't!'

She sat down on the folding-stool beside the cot, and after a while put her hand on his. He tried to pull away, but lacked the strength.

A long silence fell between them.

'Osden,' she murmured, 'I'm sorry. I'm very sorry. I will you well. Let me will you well, Osden. I don't want to hurt you. Listen, I do see now. It was one of us. That's right, isn't it. No, don't answer, only tell me if I'm wrong; but I'm not ... Of course there are animals on this planet. Ten of them. I don't care who it was. It doesn't matter, does it. It could have been me, just now. I realize that. I didn't understand how it is, Osden. You can't see how difficult it is for us to understand ... But listen. If it were love, instead of hate and fear ... Is it never love?'

'No.'

'Why not? Why should it never be? Are human beings all so weak? That is terrible. Never mind, never mind, don't worry. Keep still. At least right now it isn't hate, is it? Sympathy at least, concern, well-wishing. You do feel that. Osden? Is it what you feel?'

'Among ... other things,' he said, almost inaudibly.

'Noise from my subconscious, I suppose. And everybody else in the room ... Listen, when we found you there in the forest,

when I tried to turn you over, you partly wakened, and I felt a horror of you. I was insane with fear for a minute. Was that your fear of me I felt?'

'No.'

Her hand was still on his, and he was quite relaxed, sinking towards sleep, like a man in pain who has been given relief from pain. 'The forest,' he muttered; she could barely understand him. 'Afraid.'

She pressed him no further, but kept her hand on his and watched him go to sleep. She knew what she felt, and what therefore he must feel. She was confident of it: there is only one emotion, or state of being, that can thus wholly reverse itself, polarize, within one moment. In Great Hainish indeed there is one word, *ontá*, for love and for hate. She was not in love with Osden, of course, that was another kettle of fish. What she felt for him was *ontá*, polarized hate. She held his hand and the current flowed between them, the tremendous electricity of touch, which he had always dreaded. As he slept the ring of anatomy-chart muscles around his mouth relaxed, and Tomiko saw on his face what none of them had ever seen, very faint, a smile. It faded. He slept on.

He was tough; next day he was sitting up, and hungry. Harfex wished to interrogate him, but Tomiko put him off. She hung a sheet of polythene over the cubicle door, as Osden himself had often done. 'Does it actually cut down your empathic reception?' she asked, and he replied, in the dry, cautious tone they were now using to each other, 'No.'

'Just a warning, then.'

'Partly. More faith-healing. Dr Hammergeld thought it worked . . . Maybe it does, a little.'

There had been love, once. A terrified child, suffocating in the tidal rush and battering of the huge emotions of adults, a drowning child, saved by one man. Taught to breathe, to live, by one man. Given everything, all protection and love, by one man. Father/Mother/God: no other. 'Is he still alive?' Tomiko asked, thinking of Osden's incredible loneliness, and

the strange cruelty of the great doctors. She was shocked when she heard his forced, tinny laugh. 'He died at least two and a half centuries ago,' Osden said. 'Do you forget where we are, Coordinator? We've all left our little families behind . . .'

Outside the polythene curtain the eight other human beings on World 4470 moved vaguely. Their voices were low and strained. Eskwana slept; Poswet To was in therapy; Jenny Chong was trying to rig lights in her cubicle so that she wouldn't cast a shadow.

'They're all scared,' Tomiko said, scared. 'They've all got these ideas about what attacked you. A sort of ape-potato, a giant fanged spinach, I don't know . . . Even Harfex. You may be right not to force them to see. That would be worse, to lose confidence in one another. But why are we all so shaky, unable to face the fact, going to pieces so easily? Are we really all insane?'

'We'll soon be more so.'

'Why?'

'There *is* something.' He closed his mouth, the muscles of his lips stood out rigid.

'Something sentient?'

'A sentience.'

'In the forest?'

He nodded.

'What is it, then—?'

'The fear.' He began to look strained again, and moved restlessly. 'When I fell, there, you know, I didn't lose consciousness at once. Or I kept regaining it. I don't know. It was more like being paralyzed.'

'You were.'

'I was on the ground. I couldn't get up. My face was in the dirt, in that soft leaf mold. It was in my nostrils and eyes. I couldn't move. Couldn't see. As if I was in the ground. Sunk into it, part of it. I knew I was between two trees even though I never saw them. I suppose I could feel the roots. Below me in the ground, down under the ground. My hands were bloody, I could feel that, and the blood made the dirt around my face

sticky. I felt the fear. It kept growing. As if they'd finally *known* I was there, lying on them there, under them, among them, the thing they feared, and yet part of their fear itself. I couldn't stop sending the fear back, and it kept growing, and I couldn't move, I couldn't get away. I would pass out, I think, and then the fear would bring me to again, and I still couldn't move. Any more than they can.'

Tomiko felt the cold stirring of her hair, the readying of the apparatus of terror. 'They: who are they, Osden?'

'They, it – I don't know. The fear.'

'What is he talking about?' Harfex demanded when Tomiko reported this conversation. She would not let Harfex question Osden yet, feeling that she must protect Osden from the onslaught of the Hainishman's powerful, over-repressed emotions. Unfortunately this fueled the slow fire of paranoid anxiety that burned in poor Harfex, and he thought she and Osden were in league, hiding some fact of great importance or peril from the rest of the team.

'It's like the blind man trying to describe the elephant. Osden hasn't seen or heard the . . . the sentience, any more than we have.'

'But he's felt it, my dear Haito,' Harfex said with just-suppressed rage. 'Not empathically. On his skull. It came and knocked him down and beat him with a blunt instrument. Did he not catch *one* glimpse of it?'

'What would he have seen, Harfex?' Tomiko asked, but he would not hear her meaningful tone; even he had blocked out that comprehension. What one fears is alien. The murderer is an outsider, a foreigner, not one of us. The evil is not in me!

'The first blow knocked him pretty well out,' Tomiko said a little wearily, 'he didn't see anything. But when he came to again, alone in the forest, he felt a great fear. Not his own fear, an empathic effect. He is certain of that. And certain it was nothing picked up from any of us. So that evidently the native life-forms are not all insentient.'

Harfex looked at her a moment, grim. 'You're trying to

frighten me, Haito. I do not understand your motives.' He got up and went off to his laboratory table, walking slowly and stiffly, like a man of eighty not of forty.

She looked round at the others. She felt some desperation. Her new, fragile, and profound interdependence with Osden gave her, she was well aware, some added strength. But if even Harfex could not keep his head, who of the others would? Porlock and Eskwana were shut in their cubicles, the others were all working or busy with something. There was something queer about their positions. For a while the Coordinator could not tell what it was, then she saw that they were all sitting facing the nearby forest. Playing chess with Asnanifoil, Olleroo had edged her chair around until it was almost beside his.

She went to Mannon, who was dissecting a tangle of spidery brown roots, and told him to look for the pattern-puzzle. He saw it at once, and said with unusual brevity, 'Keeping an eye on the enemy.'

'What enemy? What do *you* feel, Mannon?' She had a sudden hope in him as a psychologist, on this obscure ground of hints and empathies where biologists went astray.

'I feel a strong anxiety with a specific spatial orientation. But I am not an empath. Therefore the anxiety is explicable in terms of the particular stress-situation, that is, the attack on a team member in the forest, and also in terms of the total stress-situation, that is, my presence in a totally alien environment, for which the archetypical connotations of the word "forest" provide an inevitable metaphor.'

Hours later Tomiko woke to hear Osden screaming in nightmare; Mannon was calming him, and she sank back into her own dark-branching pathless dreams. In the morning Eskwana did not wake. He could not be roused with stimulant drugs. He clung to his sleep, slipping farther and farther back, mumbling softly now and then until, wholly regressed, he lay curled on his side, thumb at his lips, gone.

'Two days; two down. Ten little Indians, nine little Indians . . .' That was Porlock.

'And you're the next little Indian,' Jenny Chong snapped. 'Go analyze your urine, Porlock!'

'He is driving us all insane,' Porlock said, getting up and waving his left arm. 'Can't you feel it? For God's sake, are you all deaf and blind? Can't you feel what he's doing, the emanations? It all comes from him – from his room there – from his mind. He is driving us all insane with fear!'

'Who is?' said Asnanifoil, looming precipitous and hairy over the little Terran.

'Do I have to say his name? Osden, then. Osden! Osden! Why do you think I tried to kill him? In self-defense! To save all of us! Because you won't see what he's doing to us. He's sabotaged the mission by making us quarrel, and now he's going to drive us all insane by projecting fear at us so that we can't sleep or think, like a huge radio that doesn't make any sound, but it broadcasts all the time, and you can't sleep, and you can't think. Haito and Harfex are already under his control but the rest of you can be saved. I had to do it!'

'You didn't do it very well,' Osden said, standing half-naked, all rib and bandage, at the door of his cubicle. 'I could have hit myself harder. Hell, it isn't me that's scaring you blind, Porlock, it's out there – there, in the woods!'

Porlock made an ineffectual attempt to assault Osden; Asnanifoil held him back, and continued to hold him effortlessly while Mannon gave him a sedative shot. He was put away shouting about giant radios. In a minute the sedative took effect, and he joined a peaceful silence to Eskwana's.

'All right,' said Harfex. 'Now, Osden, you'll tell us what you know and all you know.'

Osden said, 'I don't know anything.'

He looked battered and faint. Tomiko made him sit down before he talked.

'After I'd been three days in the forest, I thought I was occasionally receiving some kind of affect.'

'Why didn't you report it?'

'Thought I was going spla, like the rest of you.'

'That, equally, should have been reported.'

'You'd have called me back to base. I couldn't take it. You realize that my inclusion in the mission was a bad mistake. I'm not able to coexist with nine other neurotic personalities at close quarters. I was wrong to volunteer for Extreme Survey, and the Authority was wrong to accept me.'

No one spoke; but Tomiko saw, with certainty this time, the flinch in Osden's shoulders and the tightening of his facial muscles, as he registered their bitter agreement.

'Anyhow, I didn't want to come back to base because I was curious. Even going psycho, how could I pick up empathic affects when there was no creature to emit them? They weren't bad, then. Very vague. Queer. Like a draft in a closed room, a flicker in the corner of your eye. Nothing really.'

For a moment he had been borne up on their listening; they heard, so he spoke. He was wholly at their mercy. If they disliked him he had to be hateful; if they mocked him he became grotesque; if they listened to him he was the storyteller. He was helplessly obedient to the demands of their emotions, reactions, moods. And there were seven of them, too many to cope with, so that he must be constantly knocked about from one to another's whim. He could not find coherence. Even as he spoke and held them, somebody's attention would wander: Olleroo perhaps was thinking that he wasn't unattractive, Harfex was seeking the ulterior motive of his words, Asnanifoil's mind, which could not be long held by the concrete, was roaming off towards the eternal peace of number, and Tomiko was distracted by pity, by fear. Osden's voice faltered. He lost the thread. 'I . . . I thought it must be the trees,' he said, and stopped.

'It's not the trees,' Harfex said. 'They have no more nervous system than do plants of the Hainish Descent on Earth. None.'

'You're not seeing the forest for the trees, as they say on Earth,' Mannon put in, smiling elfinly; Harfex stared at him. 'What about those root-nodes we've been puzzling about for twenty days – eh?'

'What about them?'

'They are, indubitably, connections. Connections among the trees. Right? Now let's just suppose, most improbably, that you knew nothing of animal brain-structure. And you were given one axon, or one detached glial cell, to examine. Would you be likely to discover what it was? Would you see that the cell was capable of sentience?'

'No. Because it isn't. A single cell is capable of mechanical response to stimulus. No more. Are you hypothesizing that individual arboriformes are "cells" in a kind of brain, Mannon?'

'Not exactly. I'm merely pointing out that they are all interconnected, both by the root-node linkage and by your green epiphytes in the branches. A linkage of incredible complexity and physical extent. Why, even the prairie grass-forms have those root-connectors, don't they? I know that sentience or intelligence isn't a thing, you can't find it in, or analyze it out from, the cells of a brain. It's a function of the connected cells. It is, in a sense, the connection: the connectedness. It doesn't exist. I'm not trying to say it exists. I'm only guessing that Osden might be able to describe it.'

And Osden took him up, speaking as if in trance. 'Sentience without senses. Blind, deaf, nerveless, moveless. Some irritability, response to touch. Response to sun, to light, to water, and chemicals in the earth around the roots. Nothing comprehensible to an animal mind. Presence without mind. Awareness of being, without object or subject. Nirvana.'

'Then why do you receive fear?' Tomiko asked in a low voice.

'I don't know. I can't see how awareness of objects, of others, could arise: an unperceiving response ... But there was an uneasiness, for days. And then when I lay between the two trees and my blood was on their roots—' Osden's face glittered with sweat. 'It became fear,' he said shrilly, 'only fear.'

'If such a function existed,' Harfex said, 'it would not be capable of conceiving of a self-moving, material entity, or

responding to one. It could no more become aware of us than we can "become aware" of Infinity.'

'"The silence of those infinite expanses terrifies me",' muttered Tomiko. 'Pascal was aware of Infinity. By way of fear.'

'To a forest,' Mannon said, 'we might appear as forest fires. Hurricanes. Dangers. What moves quickly is dangerous, to a plant. The rootless would be alien, terrible. And if it is mind, it seems only too probable that it might become aware of Osden, whose own mind is open to connection with all others so long as he's conscious, and who was lying in pain and afraid within it, actually inside it. No wonder it was afraid—'

'Not "it",' Harfex said. 'There is no being, no huge creature, no person! There could at most be only a function—'

'There is only a fear,' Osden said.

They were all still a while, and heard the stillness outside.

'Is that what I feel all the time coming up behind me?' Jenny Chong asked, subdued.

Osden nodded. 'You all feel it, deaf as you are. Eskwana's the worst off, because he actually has some empathic capacity. He could send if he learned how, but he's too weak, never will be anything but a medium.'

'Listen, Osden,' Tomiko said, 'you can send. Then send to it – the forest, the fear out there – tell it that we won't hurt it. Since it has, or is, some sort of affect that translates into what we feel as emotion, can't you translate back? Send out a message, We are harmless, we are friendly.'

'You must know that nobody can emit a false empathic message, Haito. You can't send something that doesn't exist.'

'But we don't intend harm, we are friendly.'

'Are we? In the forest, when you picked me up, did you feel friendly?'

'No. Terrified. But that's – it, the forest, the plants, not my own fear, isn't it?'

'What's the difference? It's all you felt. Can't you see,' and Osden's voice rose in exasperation, 'why I dislike you and you

dislike me, all of you? Can't you see that I retransmit every negative or aggressive affect you've felt towards me since we first met? I return your hostility, with thanks. I do it in self-defense. Like Porlock. It is self-defense, though; it's the only technique I developed to replace my original defense of total withdrawal from others. Unfortunately it creates a closed circuit, self-sustaining and self-reinforcing. Your initial reaction to me was the instinctive antipathy to a cripple; by now of course it's hatred. Can you fail to see my point? The forest-mind out there transmits only terror, now, and the only message I can send it is terror, because when exposed to it I can feel nothing except terror!'

'What must we do, then?' said Tomiko, and Mannon replied promptly, 'Move camp. To another continent. If there are plant-minds there, they'll be slow to notice us, as this one was; maybe they won't notice us at all.'

'It would be a considerable relief,' Osden observed stiffly. The others had been watching him with a new curiosity. He had revealed himself, they had seen him as he was, a helpless man in a trap. Perhaps, like Tomiko, they had seen that the trap itself, his crass and cruel egotism, was their own construction, not his. They had built the cage and locked him in it, and like a caged ape he threw filth out through the bars. If, meeting him, they had offered trust, if they had been strong enough to offer him love, how might he have appeared to them?

None of them could have done so, and it was too late now. Given time, given solitude, Tomiko might have built up with him a slow resonance of feeling, a consonance of trust, a harmony; but there was no time, their job must be done. There was not room enough for the cultivation of so great a thing, and they must make do with sympathy, with pity, the small change of love. Even that much had given her strength, but it was nowhere near enough for him. She could see in his flayed face now his savage resentment of their curiosity, even of her pity.

'Go lie down, that gash is bleeding again,' she said, and he obeyed her.

Next morning they packed up, melted down the sprayform hangar and living quarters, lifted *Gum* on mechanical drive and took her halfway round World 4470, over the red and green lands, the many warm green seas. They had picked out a likely spot on Continent G: a prairie, twenty thousand square kilos of windswept graminiformes. No forest was within a hundred kilos of the site, and there were no lone trees or groves on the plain. The plant-forms occurred only in large species-colonies, never intermingled, except for certain tiny ubiquitous saprophytes and spore-bearers. The team sprayed holomeld over structure forms, and by evening of the thirty-two-hour day were settled in to the new camp. Eskwana was still asleep and Porlock still sedated, but everyone else was cheerful. 'You can breathe here!' they kept saying.

Osden got on his feet and went shakily to the doorway; leaning there he looked through twilight over the dim reaches of the swaying grass that was not grass. There was a faint, sweet odor of pollen on the wind; no sound but the soft, vast sibilance of wind. His bandaged head cocked a little, the empath stood motionless for a long time. Darkness came, and the stars, lights in the windows of the distant house of Man. The wind had ceased, there was no sound. He listened.

In the long night Haito Tomiko listened. She lay still and heard the blood in her arteries, the breathing of sleepers, the wind blowing, the dark veins running, the dreams advancing, the vast static of stars increasing as the universe died slowly, the sound of death walking. She struggled out of her bed, fled the tiny solitude of her cubicle. Eskwana alone slept. Porlock lay straitjacketed, raving softly in his obscure native tongue. Olleroo and Jenny Chong were playing cards, grim-faced. Poswet To was in the therapy niche, plugged in. Asnanifoil was drawing a mandala, the Third Pattern of the Primes. Mannon and Harfex were sitting up with Osden.

She changed the bandages on Osden's head. His lank, reddish hair, where she had not had to shave it, looked strange. It was salted with white, now. Her hands shook as she worked.

Nobody had yet said anything.

'How can the fear be here too?' she said, and her voice rang flat and false in the terrific silence.

'It's not just the trees; the grasses too . . .'

'But we're twelve thousand kilos from where we were this morning, we left it on the other side of the planet.'

'It's all one,' Osden said. 'One big green thought. How long does it take a thought to get from one side of your brain to the other?'

'It doesn't think. It isn't thinking,' Harfex said, lifelessly. 'It's merely a network of processes. The branches, the epiphytic growths, the roots with those nodal junctures between individuals: they must all be capable of transmitting electro-chemical impulses. There are no individual plants, then, properly speaking. Even the pollen is part of the linkage, no doubt, a sort of windborne sentience, connecting overseas. But it is not conceivable. That all the biosphere of a planet should be one network of communications, sensitive, irrational, immortal, isolated . . .'

'Isolated', said Osden. 'That's it! That's the fear. It isn't that we're motile, or destructive. It's just that we are. We are other. There has never been any other.'

'You're right,' Mannon said, almost whispering. 'It has no peers. No enemies. No relationship with anything but itself. One alone forever.'

'Then what's the function of its intelligence in species-survival?'

'None, maybe,' Osden said. 'Why are you getting tele-ological, Harfex? Aren't you a Hainishman? Isn't the measure of complexity the measure of the eternal joy?'

Harfex did not take the bait. He looked ill. 'We should leave this world,' he said.

'Now you know why I always want to get out, get away from you,' Osden said with a kind of morbid geniality. 'It isn't pleasant, is it – the other's fear . . .? If only it were an animal intelligence. I can get through to animals. I get along with

cobras and tigers; superior intelligence gives one the advantage. I should have been used in a zoo, not on a human team . . . If I could get through to the damned stupid potato! If it wasn't so overwhelming . . . I still pick up more than the fear, you know. And before it panicked it had a – there was a serenity. I couldn't take it in, then, I didn't realize how big it was. To know the whole daylight, after all, and the whole night. All the winds and lulls together. The winter stars and the summer stars at the same time. To have roots, and no enemies. To be entire. Do you see? No invasion. No others. To be whole . . .'

He had never spoken before, Tomiko thought.

'You are defenseless against it, Osden,' she said. 'Your personality has changed already. You're vulnerable to it. We may not all go mad, but you will, if we don't leave.'

He hesitated, then he looked up at Tomiko, the first time he had ever met her eyes, a long, still look, clear as water.

'What's sanity ever done for me?' he said, mocking. 'But you have a point, Haito. You have something there.'

'We should get away,' Harfex muttered.

'If I gave in to it,' Osden mused, 'could I communicate?'

'By "give in",' Mannon said in a rapid, nervous voice, 'I assume that you mean, stop sending back the empathic information which you receive from the plant-entity: stop rejecting the fear, and absorb it. That will either kill you at once, or drive you back into total psychological withdrawal, autism.'

'Why?' said Osden. 'Its message is *rejection*. But my salvation is rejection. It's not intelligent. But I am.'

'The scale is wrong. What can a single human brain achieve against something so vast?'

'A single human brain can perceive pattern on the scale of stars and galaxies,' Tomiko said, 'and interpret it as Love.'

Mannon looked from one to the other of them; Harfex was silent.

'It'd be easier in the forest,' Osden said. 'Which of you will fly me over?'

'When?'

'Now. Before you all crack up or go violent.'

'I will,' Tomiko said.

'None of us will,' Harfex said.

'I can't,' Mannon said. 'I . . . I am too frightened. I'd crash the jet.'

'Bring Eskwana along. If I can pull this off, he might serve as a medium.'

'Are you accepting the Sensor's plan, Coordinator?' Harfex asked formally.

'Yes.'

'I disapprove. I will come with you, however.'

'I think we're compelled, Harfex,' Tomiko said, looking at Osden's face, the ugly white mask transfigured, eager as a lover's face.

Olleroo and Jenny Chong, playing cards to keep their thoughts from their haunted beds, their mounting dread, chattered like scared children. 'This thing, it's in the forest, it'll get you—'

'Scared of the dark?' Osden jeered.

'But look at Eskwana, and Porlock, and even Asnanifoil—'

'It can't hurt you. It's an impulse passing through synapses, a wind passing through branches. It is only a nightmare.'

They took off in a helijet, Eskwana curled up still sound asleep in the rear compartment, Tomiko piloting, Harfex and Osden silent, watching ahead for the dark line of forest across the vague grey miles of starlit plain.

They neared the black line, crossed it; now under them was darkness.

She sought a landing place, flying low, though she had to fight her frantic wish to fly high, to get out, get away. The huge vitality of the plant-world was far stronger here in the forest, and its panic beat in immense dark waves. There was a pale patch ahead, a bare knoll-top a little higher than the tallest of the black shapes around it; the not-trees; the rooted; the parts of the whole. She set the helijet down in the glade, a bad land-

ing. Her hands on the stick were slippery, as if she had rubbed them with cold soap.

About them now stood the forest, black in darkness.

Tomiko cowered and shut her eyes. Eskwana moaned in his sleep. Harfex's breath came short and loud, and he sat rigid, even when Osden reached across him and slid the door open.

Osden stood up; his back and bandaged head were just visible in the dim glow of the control panel as he paused stooping in the doorway.

Tomiko was shaking. She could not raise her head. 'No, no, no, no, no, no, no,' she said in a whisper. 'No. No. No.'

Osden moved suddenly and quietly, swinging out of the doorway, down into the dark. He was gone.

I am coming! said a great voice that made no sound.

Tomiko screamed. Harfex coughed; he seemed to be trying to stand up, but did not do so.

Tomiko drew in upon herself, all centered in the blind eye in her belly, in the center of her being; and outside that there was nothing but the fear.

It ceased.

She raised her head; slowly unclenched her hands. She sat up straight. The night was dark, and stars shone over the forest. There was nothing else.

'Osden,' she said, but her voice would not come. She spoke again, louder, a lone bullfrog croak. There was no reply.

She began to realize that something had gone wrong with Harfex. She was trying to find his head in the darkness, for he had slipped down from the seat, when all at once, in the dead quiet, in the dark rear compartment of the craft, a voice spoke. 'Good', it said.

It was Eskwana's voice. She snapped on the interior lights and saw the engineer lying curled up asleep, his hand half over his mouth.

The mouth opened and spoke. 'All well,' it said.

'Osden—'

'All well,' said the soft voice from Eskwana's mouth.

'Where are you?'

Silence.

'Come back.'

A wind was rising. 'I'll stay here,' the soft voice said.

'You can't stay—'

Silence.

'You'd be alone, Osden!'

'Listen'. The voice was fainter, slurred, as if lost in the sound of wind. 'Listen. I will you well.'

She called his name after that, but there was no answer. Eskwana lay still. Harfex lay stiller.

'Osden!' she cried, leaning out the doorway into the dark, windshaken silence of the forest of being. 'I will come back. I must get Harfex to the base. I will come back, Osden!'

Silence and wind in leaves.

They finished the prescribed survey of World 4470, the eight of them; it took them forty-one days more. Asnanifoil and one or another of the women went into the forest daily at first, searching for Osden in the region around the bare knoll, though Tomiko was not in her heart sure which bare knoll they had landed on that night in the very heart and vortex of terror. They left piles of supplies for Osden, food enough for fifty years, clothing, tents, tools. They did not go on searching; there was no way to find a man alone, hiding, if he wanted to hide, in those unending labyrinths and dim corridors vine-entangled, root-floored. They might have passed within arm's reach of him and never seen him.

But he was there; for there was no fear any more.

Rational, and valuing reason more highly after an intolerable experience of the immortal mindless, Tomiko tried to understand rationally what Osden had done. But the words escaped her control. He had taken the fear into himself, and, accepting, had transcended it. He had given up his self to the alien, an unreserved surrender, that left no place for evil. He

had learned the love of the Other, and thereby had been given his whole self. —But this is not the vocabulary of reason.

The people of the Survey team walked under the trees, through the vast colonies of life, surrounded by a dreaming silence, a brooding calm that was half aware of them and wholly indifferent to them. There were no hours. Distance was no matter. Had we but world enough and time ... The planet turned between the sunlight and the great dark; winds of winter and summer blew fine, pale pollen across the quiet seas.

Gum returned after many surveys, years, and lightyears, to what had several centuries ago been Smeming Port. There were still men there, to receive (incredulously) the team's reports, and to record its losses: Biologist Harfex, dead of fear, and Sensor Osden, left as a colonist.

THE STARS BELOW

The popular notion of science fiction, I guess, is of a story that takes some possible or impossible technological gimmick-of-the-future – Soylent Green, the time machine, the submarine – and makes hay out of it. There certainly are science fiction stories which do just that, but to define science fiction by them is a bit like defining the United States as Kansas.

Writing 'The Stars Below', I thought I knew what I was doing. As in the early story 'The Masters', I was telling a story not about a gimmick or device or hypothesis, but about science itself – the idea of science. And about what happens to the idea of science when it meets utterly opposed and powerful ideas, embodied in government, as when seventeenth-century astronomy ran up against the Pope, or genetics in the 1930s ran up against Stalin. But all this was cast as' a psychomyth, a story outside real time, past or future, in part to generalize it, and in part because I was also using science as a synonym for art. What happens to the creative mind when it is driven underground?

That was the question, and I thought I knew my answer. It all seemed straightforward, a mere allegory, really. But you don't go exploring the places underground all that easily. The symbols you thought were simple equivalences, signs, come alive, and take on meanings you did not intend and cannot explain. Long after I wrote the story I came on a passage in Jung's On the Nature of the Psyche: *'We would do well to think of ego-consciousness as being surrounded by a multitude of little luminosities . . . Introspective intuitions . . ; capture the state of the unconscious: The star-strewn heavens, stars*

reflected in dark water, nuggets of gold or golden sand scattered in black earth.' And he quotes from an alchemist, 'Seminate aurum in terram albam foliatam'—the precious metal strewn in the layers of white clay.

Perhaps this story is not about science, or about art, but about the mind, my mind, any mind, that turns inward to itself.

The wooden house and outbuildings caught fire fast, blazed up, burned down, but the dome, built of lathe and plaster above a drum of brick, would not burn. What they did at last was heap up the wreckage of the telescopes, the instruments, the books and charts and drawings, in the middle of the floor under the dome, pour oil on the heap, and set fire to that. The flames spread to the wooden beams of the big telescope frame and to the clockwork mechanisms. Villagers watching from the foot of the hill saw the dome, whitish against the green evening sky, shudder and turn, first in one direction then in the other, while a black and yellow smoke full of sparks gushed from the oblong slit: an ugly and uncanny thing to see.

It was getting dark, stars were showing in the east. Orders were shouted. The soldiers came down the road in single file, dark men in dark harness, silent.

The villagers at the foot of the hill stayed on after the soldiers had gone. In a life without change or breadth a fire is as good as a festival. They did not climb the hill, and as the night grew full dark they drew closer together. After a while they began to go back to their villages. Some looked back over their shoulders at the hill, where nothing moved. The stars turned slowly behind the black beehive of the dome, but it did not turn to follow them.

About an hour before daybreak a man rode up the steep zigzag, dismounted by the ruins of the workshops, and approached the dome on foot. The door had been smashed in. Through it a reddish haze of light was visible, very dim, coming from a massive support-beam that had fallen and had smoldered all night inward to its core. A hanging, sour smoke

thickened the air inside the dome. A tall figure moved there and its shadow moved with it, cast upward on the murk. Sometimes it stooped, or stopped, then blundered slowly on.

The man at the door said: 'Guennar! Master Guennar!'

The man in the dome stopped still, looking towards the door. He had just picked up something from the mess of wreckage and half-burnt stuff on the floor. He put this object mechanically into his coat pocket, still peering at the door. He came towards it. His eyes were red and swollen almost shut, he breathed harshly in gasps, his hair and clothes were scorched and smeared with black ash.

'Where were you?'

The man in the dome pointed vaguely at the ground.

'There's a cellar? That's where you were during the fire? By God! Gone to ground! I knew it, I knew you'd be here.' Bord laughed, a little crazily, taking Guennar's arm. 'Come on. Come out of there, for the love of God. There's light in the east already.'

The astronomer came reluctantly, looking not at the gray east but back up at the slit in the dome, where a few stars burned clear. Bord pulled him outside, made him mount the horse, and then, bridle in hand, set off down the hill leading the horse at a fast walk.

The astronomer held the pommel with one hand. The other hand, which had been burned across the palm and fingers when he picked up a metal fragment still red-hot under its coat of cinders, he kept pressed againt his thigh. He was not conscious of doing so, or of the pain. Sometimes his senses told him, 'I am on horseback', or 'It's getting lighter', but there fragmentary messages made no sense to him. He shivered with cold as the dawn wind rose, rattling the dark woods by which the two men and the horse now passed in a deep lane overhung by teasel and briar; but the woods, the wind, the whitening sky, the cold were all remote from his mind, in which there was nothing but a darkness shot with the reek and heat of burning.

Bord made him dismount. There was sunlight around them

now, lying long on rocks above a river valley. There was a dark place, and Bord urged him and pulled him into the dark place. It was not hot and close there but cold and silent. As soon as Bord let him stop he sank down, for his knees would not bear; and he felt the cold rock against his seared and throbbing hands.

'Gone to earth, by God!' said Bord, looking about at the veined walls, marked with the scars of miners' picks, in the light of his lanterned candle. 'I'll be back; after dark, maybe. Don't come out. Don't go farther in. This is an old adit, they haven't worked this end of the mine for years. May be slips and pitfalls in these old tunnels. Don't come out! Lie low. When the hounds are gone, we'll run you across the border.'

Bord turned and went back up the adit in darkness. When the sound of his steps had long since died away, the astronomer lifted his head and looked around him at the dark walls and the little burning candle. Presently he blew it out. There came upon him the earth-smelling darkness, silent and complete. He saw green shapes, ocherous blots drifting on the black; these faded slowly. The dull, chill black was balm to his inflamed and aching eyes, and to his mind.

If he thought, sitting there in the dark, his thoughts found no words. He was feverish from exhaustion and smoke inhalation and a few slight burns, and in an abnormal condition of mind; but perhaps his mind's workings, though lucid and serene, had never been normal. It is not normal for a man to spend twenty years grinding lenses, building telescopes, peering at stars, making calculations, lists, maps and charts of things which no one knows or cares about, things which cannot be reached, or touched, or held. And now all he had spent his life on was gone, burned. What was left of him might as well be, as it was, buried.

But it did not occur to him, this idea of being buried. All he was keenly aware of was a great burden of anger and grief, a burden he was unfit to carry. It was crushing his mind, crushing out reason. And the darkness here seemed to relieve that

pressure. He was accustomed to the dark, he had lived at night. The weight here was only rock, only earth. No granite is so hard as hatred and no clay so cold as cruelty. The earth's black innocence enfolded him. He lay down within it, trembling a little with pain and with relief from pain, and slept.

Light waked him. Count Bord was there, lighting the candle with flint and steel. Bord's face was vivid in the light: the high color and blue eyes of a keen huntsman, a red mouth, sensual and obstinate. 'They're on the scent,' he was saying. 'They know you got away.'

'Why . . .' said the astronomer. His voice was weak; his throat, like his eyes, was still smoke-inflamed. 'Why are they after me?'

'Why? Do you still need telling? To burn you alive, man! For heresy!' Bord's blue eyes glared through the steadying glow of the candle.

'But it's gone, burned, all I did.'

'Aye, the earth's stopped, all right, but where's their fox? They want their fox! But damned if I'll let them get you.'

The astronomer's eyes, light and wide-set, met his and held. 'Why?'

'You think I'm a fool,' Bord said with a grin that was not a smile, a wolf's grin, the grin of the hunted and the hunter. 'And I am one. I was a fool to warn you. You never listened. I was a fool to listen to you. But I liked to listen to you. I liked to hear you talk about the stars and the courses of the planets and the ends of time. Who else ever talked to me of anything but seed corn and cow dung? Do you see? And I don't like soldiers and strangers, and trials and burnings. Your truth, their truth, what do I know about the truth? Am I a master? Do I know the courses of the stars? Maybe you do. Maybe they do. All I know is you have sat at my table and talked to me. Am I to watch you burn? God's fire, they say; but you said the stars are the fires of God. Why do you ask me that, "Why?" Why do you ask a fool's question of a fool?'

'I am sorry,' the astronomer said.

'What do you know about men?' the count said. 'You thought they'd let you be. And you thought I'd let you burn.' He looked at Guennar through the candlelight, grinning like a driven wolf, but in his blue eyes there was a glint of real amusement. 'We who live down on the earth, you see, not up among the stars . . .'

He had brought a tinderbox and three tallow candles, a bottle of water, a ball of peas-pudding, a sack of bread. He left soon, warning the astronomer again not to venture out of the mine.

When Guennar woke again a strangeness in his situation troubled him, not one which would have worried most people hiding in a hole to save their skins, but most distressing to him: he did not know the time.

It was not clocks he missed, the sweet banging of the church bells in the villages calling to morning and evening prayer, the delicate and willing accuracy of the timepiece he used in his observatory and on whose refinement so many of his discoveries had depended; it was not the clocks he missed, but the great clock.

Not seeing the sky, one cannot know the turning of the earth. All the processes of time, the sun's bright arch and the moon's phases, the planet's dance, the wheeling of the constellations around the pole star, the vaster wheeling of the seasons of the stars, all these were lost, the warp on which his life was woven.

Here there was no time.

'O my God,' Guennar the astronomer prayed in the darkness under ground, 'how can it offend you to be praised? All I ever saw in my telescopes was one spark of your glory, one least fragment of the order of your creation. You could not be jealous of that, my Lord! And there were few enough who believed me, even so. Was it my arrogance in daring to describe your works? But how could I help it, Lord, when you let me see the endless fields of stars? Could I see and be silent? O my God, do not punish me any more, let me rebuild the smaller telescope. I will not speak, I will not publish, if it troubles your holy Church. I

will not say anything more about the orbits of the planets or the nature of the stars. I will not speak, Lord, only let me see!'

'What the devil, be quiet, Master Guennar. I could hear you halfway up the tunnel,' said Bord, and the astronomer opened his eyes to the dazzle of Bord's lantern. 'They've called the full hunt up for you. Now you're a necromancer. They swear they saw you sleeping in your house when they came, and they barred the doors; but there's no bones in the ashes.'

'I was asleep,' Guennar said, covering his eyes. 'They came, the soldiers . . . I should have listened to you. I went into the passage under the dome. I left a passage there so I could go back to the hearth on cold nights, when it's cold my fingers get too stiff, I have to go warm my hands sometimes.' He spread out his blistered, blackened hands and looked at them vaguely. 'Then I heard them overhead . . .'

'Here's some more food. What the devil, haven't you eaten?'

'Has it been long?'

'A night and a day. It's night now. Raining. Listen, Master: there's two of the black hounds living at my house now. Emissaries of the Council, what the devil, I had to offer hospitality. This is my county, they're here, I'm the count. It makes it hard for me to come. And I don't want to send any of my people here. What if the priests asked them, 'Do you know where he is? Will you answer to God you don't know where he is?' It's best they don't know. I'll come when I can. You're all right here? You'll stay here? I'll get you out of here and over the border when they've cleared away. They're like flies now. Don't talk aloud like that. They might look into these old tunnels. You should go farther in. I will come back. Stay with God, Master.'

'Go with God, count.'

He saw the color of Bord's blue eyes, the leap of shadows up the rough-hewn roof as he took up the lantern and turned away. Light and color died as Bord, at the turning, put out the lantern. Guennar heard him stumble and swear as he groped his way.

Presently Guennar lighted one of his candles and ate and drank a little, eating the staler bread first, and breaking off a piece of the crusted lump of peas-pudding. This time Bord had brought him three loaves and some salt meat, two more candles and a second skin bottle of water, and a heavy duffle cloak. Guennar had not felt cold. He was wearing the coat he always wore on cold nights in the observatory and very often slept in, when he came stumbling to bed at dawn. It was a good sheepskin, filthy from his rummagings in the wreckage in the dome and scorched at the sleeve-ends, but it was as warm as ever, and was like his own skin to him. He sat inside it eating, gazing out through the sphere of frail yellow candlelight to the darkness of the tunnel beyond. Bord's words, 'You should go farther in,' were in his mind. When he was done eating he bundled up the provisions in the cloak, took up the bundle in one hand and the lighted candle in the other, and set off down the side-tunnel and then the adit, down and inward.

After a few hundred paces he came to a major cross-tunnel, off which ran many short leads and some large rooms or stopes. He turned left, and presently passed a big stope in three levels. He entered it. The farthest level was only about five feet under the roof, which was still well timbered with posts and beams. In a corner of the backmost level, behind an angle of quartz intrusion which the miners had left jutting out as a supporting buttress, he made his new camp, setting out the food, water, tinderbox, and candles where they would come under his hand easily in the dark, and laying the cloak as a mattress on the floor, which was of a rubbly, hard clay. Then he put out the candle, already burned down by a quarter of its length, and lay down in the dark.

After his third return to that first side-tunnel, finding no sign that Bord had come there, he went back to his camp and studied his provisions. There were still two loaves of bread, half a bottle of water, and the salt meat, which he had not yet touched; and four candles. He guessed that it might have been

six days since Bord had come, but it might have been three, or eight. He was thirsty, but dared not drink, so long as he had no other supply.

He set off to find water.

At first he counted his paces. After a hundred and twenty he saw that the timbering of the tunnel was askew, and there were places where the rubble fill had broken through, half filling the passage. He came to a winze, a vertical shaft, easy to scramble down by what remained of the wooden ladder, but after it, in the lower level, he forgot to count his steps. Once he passed a broken pick handle; farther on he saw a miner's discarded headband, a stump of candle still stuck in the forehead socket. He dropped this into the pocket of his coat and went on.

The monotony of the walls of hewn stone and planking dulled his mind. He walked on like one who will walk forever. Darkness followed him and went ahead of him.

His candle burning short spilled a stream of hot tallow on his fingers, hurting him. He dropped the candle, and it went out.

He groped for it in the sudden dark, sickened by the reek of its smoke, lifting his head to avoid that stink of burning. Before him, straight before him, far away, he saw the stars.

Tiny, bright, remote, caught in a narrow opening like the slot in the observatory dome: an oblong full of stars in blackness.

He got up, forgetting about the candle, and began to run towards the stars.

They moved, dancing, like the stars in the telescope field when the clockwork mechanism shuddered or when his eyes were very tired. They danced, and brightened.

He came among them, and they spoke to him.

The flames cast queer shadows on the blackened faces and brought queer lights out of the bright, living eyes.

'Here then, who's that? Hanno?'

'What were you doing up that old drift, mate?'

'Hey, who is that?'

'Who the devil, stop him—'

'Hey, mate! Hold on!'

He ran blind into the dark, back the way he had come. The lights followed him and he chased his own faint, huge shadow down the tunnel. When the shadow was swallowed by the old dark and the old silence came again he still stumbled on, stooping and groping so that he was oftenest on all fours or on his feet and one hand. At last he dropped down and lay huddled against the wall, his chest full of fire.

Silence, dark.

He found the candle end in the tin holder in his pocket, lighted it with the flint and steel, and by its glow found the vertical shaft not fifty feet from where he had stopped. He made his way back up to his camp. There he slept; woke and ate, and drank the last of his water; meant to get up and go seeking water again; fell asleep, or into a doze or daze, in which he dreamed of a voice speaking to him.

'There you are. All right. Don't startle. I'll do you no harm. I said it wasn't no knocker. Who ever heard of a knocker as tall as a man? Or who ever seen one, for that matter. They're what you *don't* see, mates, I said. And what we did see was a man, count on it. So what's he doing in the mine, said they, and what if he's a ghost, one of the lads that was caught when the house of water broke in the old south adit, maybe, come walking? Well then, I said, I'll go see that. I never seen a ghost yet, for all I heard of them. I don't care to see what's not meant to be seen, like the knocker folk, but what harm to see Temon's face again, or old Trip, haven't I seen 'em in dreams, just the same, in the ends, working away with their faces sweating same as life? Why not? So I come along. But you're no ghost, nor miner. A deserter you might be, or a thief. Or are you out of your wits, is that it, poor man? Don't fear. Hide if you like. What's it to me? There's room down here for you and me. Why are you hiding from the light of the sun?'

'The soldiers . . .'

'I thought so.'

When the old man nodded, the candle bound to his forehead set light leaping over the roof of the stope. He squatted about

ten feet from Guennar, his hands hanging between his knees. A bunch of candles and his pick, a short-handled, finely shaped tool, hung from his belt. His face and body, beneath the restless star of the candle, were rough shadows, earth-colored.

'Let me stay here.'

'Stay and welcome! Do I own the mine? Where did you come in, eh, the old drift above the river? That was luck to find that, and luck you turned this way in the crosscut, and didn't go east instead. Eastward this level goes on to the caves. There's great caves there; did you know it? Nobody knows but the miners. They opened up the caves before I was born, following the old lode that lay along here sunward. I seen the caves once, my dad took me, you should see this once, he says. See the world underneath the world. A room there was no end to. A cavern as deep as the sky, and a black stream falling into it, falling and falling till the light of the candle failed and couldn't follow it, and still the water was falling on down into the pit. The sound of it came up like a whisper without an end, out of the dark. And on beyond that there's other caves, and below. No end to them, maybe. Who knows? Cave under cave, and glittering with the barren crystal. It's all barren stone, there. And all worked out, here, years ago. It's a safe enough hole you chose, mate, if you hadn't come stumbling in on us. What was you after? Food? A human face?'

'Water.'

'No lack of that. Come on, I'll show you. Beneath here in the lower level there's all too many springs. You turned the wrong direction. I used to work down there, with the damned cold water up to my knees, before the vein ran out. A long time ago. Come on.'

The old miner left him in his camp, after showing him where the spring rose and warning him not to follow down the water-course, for the timbering would be rotted and a step or sound might bring the earth down. Down there all the timbers were covered with a deep glittering white fur, saltpeter perhaps, or a

fungus: it was very strange, above the oily water. When he was alone again Guennar thought he had dreamed that white tunnel full of black water, and the visit of the miner. When he saw a flicker of light far down the tunnel, he crouched behind the quartz buttress with a great wedge of granite in his hand: for all his fear and anger and grief had come down to one thing here in the darkness, a determination that no man would lay hand on him. A blind determination, blunt and heavy as a broken stone, heavy in his soul.

It was only the old man coming, with a hunk of dry cheese for him.

He sat with the astronomer, and talked. Guennar ate up the cheese, for he had no food left, and listened to the old man talk. As he listened the weight seemed to lift a little, he seemed to see a little farther in the dark.

'You're no common soldier,' the miner said, and he replied, 'No, I was a student once,' but no more, because he dared not tell the miner who he was. The old man knew all the events of the region; he spoke of the burning of the Round House on the hill, and of Count Bord. 'He went off to the city with them, with these blackgowns, to be tried, they do say, to come before their council. Tried for what? What did he ever do but hunt boar and deer and foxen? Is it the council of the foxen trying him? What's it all about, this snooping and soldiering and burning and trying? Better leave honest folk alone. The count was honest, as far as the rich can be, a fair landlord. But you can't trust them, none of such folk. Only down here. You can trust the men who go down into the mine. What else has a man got down here but his own hands and his mates' hands? What's between him and death, when there's a fall in the level or a winze closes and he's in the blind end, but their hands, and their shovels, and their will to dig him out? There'd be no silver up there in the sun if there wasn't trust between us down here in the dark. Down here you can count on your mates. And nobody comes but them. Can you see the owner in his lace, or the soldiers, coming down the ladders, coming down and down the

great shaft into the dark? Not them! They're brave at tramping
on the grass, but what good's a sword and shouting in the dark?
I'd like to see 'em come down here . . .'

The next time he came another man was with him, and they
brought an oil lamp and a clay jar of oil, as well as more cheese,
bread and some apples. 'It was Hanno thought of the lamp,' the
old man said. 'A hempen wick it is, if she goes out blow sharp
and she'll likely catch up again. Here's a dozen candles, too.
Young Per swiped the lot from the doler, up on the grass.'

'They all know I'm here?'

'*We* do,' the miner said briefly. '*They* don't.'

Some time after this, Guennar returned along the lower,
west-leading level he had followed before, till he saw the
miners' candles dance like stars; and he came into the stope
where they were working. They shared their meal with him.
They showed him the ways of the mine, and the pumps, and the
great shaft where the ladders were and the hanging pulleys with
their buckets; he sheered off from that, for the wind that came
sucking down the great shaft smelled to him of burning. They
took him back and let him work with them. They treated him
as a guest, as a child. They had adopted him. He was their
secret.

There is not much good spending twelve hours a day in a
black hole in the ground all your life long if there's nothing
there, no secret, no treasure, nothing hidden.

There was the silver, to be sure. But where ten crews of
fifteen had used to work these levels and there had been no end
to the groan and clatter and crash of the loaded buckets going
up on the screaming winch and the empties banging down to
meet the trammers running with their heavy carts, now one
crew of eight men worked: men over forty, old men, who had
no skill but mining. There was still some silver there in the
hard granite, in little veins among the gangue. Sometimes they
would lengthen an end by one foot in two weeks.

'It was a great mine,' they said with pride.

They showed the astronomer how to set a gad and swing the

sledge, how to go at granite with the finely balanced and sharp-pointed pick, how to sort and 'cob', what to look for, the rare bright branchings of the pure metal, the crumbling rich rock of the ore. He helped them daily. He was in the stope waiting for them when they came, and spelled one or another on and off all day with the shovel work, or sharpening tools, or running the ore-cart down its grooved plank to the great shaft, or working in the ends. There they would not let him work long; pride and habit forbade it. 'Here, leave off chopping at that like a wood-cutter. Look: this way, see?' But then another would ask him, 'Give me a blow here, lad, see, on the gad, that's it.'

They fed him from their own coarse meager meals.

In the night, alone in the hollow earth, when they had climbed the long ladders up 'to grass' as they said, he lay and thought of them, their faces, their voices, their heavy, scarred, earth-stained hands, old men's hands with thick nails blackened by bruising rock and steel; those hands, intelligent and vulnerable, which had opened up the earth and found the shining silver in the solid rock. The silver they never held, never kept, never spent. The silver that was not theirs.

'If you found a new vein, a new lode, what would you do?'

'Open her, and tell the masters.'

'Why tell the masters?'

'Why, man! We gets paid for what we brings up! D'you think we does this damned work for love?'

'Yes.'

They all laughed at him, loud, jeering laughter, innocent. The living eyes shone in their faces blackened with dust and sweat.

'Ah, if we could find a new lode! The wife would keep a pig like we had once, and by God I'd swim in beer! But if there's silver they'd have found it; that's why they pushed the work-ings so far east. But it's barren there, and worked out here, that's the short and long of it.'

Time stretched behind him and ahead of him like the dark

drifts and crosscuts of the mine, all present at once, wherever he with his small candle might be among them. When he was alone now the astronomer often wandered in the tunnels and the old stopes, knowing the dangerous places, the deep levels full of water, adept at shaky ladders and tight places, intrigued by the play of his candle on the rock walls and faces, the glitter of mica that seemed to come from deep inside the stone. Why did it sometimes shine out that way? as if the candle found something far within the shining broken surface, something that winked in answer and occulted, as if it had slipped behind a cloud or an unseen planet's disc.

'There are stars in the earth,' he thought. 'If one knew how to see them.'

Awkward with the pick, he was clever with machinery; they admired his skill, and brought him tools. He repaired pumps and windlasses; he fixed up a lamp on a chain for 'young Per' working in a long narrow deadend, with a reflector made from a tin candleholder beaten out into a curved sheet and polished with fine rock-dust and the sheepskin lining of his coat. 'It's a marvel,' Per said. 'Like daylight. Only, being behind me, it don't go out when the air gets bad, and tell me I should be backing out for a breath.'

For a man can go on working on a narrow end for some time after his candle has gone out for lack of oxygen.

'You should have a bellows rigged there.'

'What, like I was a forge?'

'Why not?'

'Do ye ever go up to the grass, nights?' asked Hanno, looking wistfully at Guennar. Hanno was a melancholy, thoughtful, soft-hearted fellow. 'Just to look about you?'

Guennar did not answer. He went off to help Bran with a timbering job; the miners did all the work that had once been done by crews of timberers, trammers, sorters, and so on.

'He's deathly afraid to leave the mine,' Per said, low.

'Just to see the stars and get a breath of the wind,' Hanno said, as if he was still speaking to Guennar.

One night the astronomer emptied out his pockets and looked at the stuff that had been in them since the night of the burning of the observatory: things he had picked up in those hours which he now could not remember, those hours when he had groped and stumbled in the smoldering wreckage, seeking . . . seeking what he had lost . . . He no longer thought of what he had lost. It was sealed off in his mind by a thick scar, a burn-scar. For a long time this scar in his mind kept him from understanding the nature of the objects now ranged before him on the dusty stone floor of the mine: a wad of papers scorched all along one side; a round piece of glass or crystal; a metal tube; a beautifully worked wooden cog-wheel; a bit of twisted blackened copper etched with fine lines; and so on, bits, wrecks, scraps. He put the papers back into his pocket, without trying to separate the brittle half-fused leaves and make out the fine script. He continued to look at and occasionally to pick up and examine the other things, especially the piece of glass.

This he knew to be the eyepiece of his ten-inch telescope. He had ground the lens himself. When he picked it up he handled it delicately, by the edges, lest the acid of his skin etch the glass. Finally he began to polish it clean, using a wisp of fine lambs-wool from his coat. When it was clear, he held it up and looked at and through it at all angles. His face was calm and intent, his light wide-set eyes steady.

Tilted in his fingers, the telescope lens reflected the lamp flame in one bright tiny point near the edge and seemingly beneath the curve of the face, as if the lens had kept a star in it from the many hundred nights it had been turned toward the sky.

He wrapped it carefully in the wisp of wool and made a place for it in the rock niche with his tinderbox. Then he took up the other things one by one.

During the next weeks the miners saw their fugitive less often while they worked. He was off a great deal by himself: exploring the deserted eastern regions of the mine, he said, when they asked him what he did.

'What for?'

'Prospecting,' he said with the brief, wincing smile that gave him a very crazy look.

'Oh, lad, what do you know about that? She's all barren there. The silver's gone; and they found no eastern lode. You might be finding a bit of poor ore or a vein of tinstone, but nothing worth the digging.'

'How do you know what's in the earth, in the rock under your feet, Per?'

'I know the signs, lad. Who should know better?'

'But if the signs are hidden?'

'Then the silver's hidden.'

'Yet you know it is there, if you knew where to dig, if you could see into the rock. And what else is there? You find the metal, because you seek it, and dig for it. But what else might you find, deeper than the mine, if you sought, if you knew where to dig?'

'Rock,' said Per. 'Rock, and rock, and rock.'

'And then?'

'And then? Hellfire, for all I know. Why else does it get hotter as the shafts go deeper? That's what they say. Getting nearer hell.'

'No,' the astronomer said, clear and firm. 'No. There is no hell beneath the rocks.'

'What is there, then, underneath it all?'

'The stars.'

'Ah,' said the miner, floored. He scratched his rough, tallow-clotted hair, and laughed. 'There's a poser,' he said, and stared at Guennar with pity and admiration. He knew Guennar was mad, but the size of his madness was a new thing to him, and admirable. 'Will you find 'em then, the stars?'

'If I learn how to look,' Guennar said, so calmly that Per had

no response but to heft his shovel and get back to loading the cart.

One morning when the miners came down they found Guennar still sleeping, rolled up in the battered cloak Count Bord had given him, and by him a strange object, a contraption made of silver tubing, tin struts and wires beaten from old headlamp-sockets, a frame of pick handles carefully carved and fitted, cogged wheels, a bit of twinkling glass. It was elusive, make-shift, delicate, crazy, intricate.

'What the devil's that?'

They stood about and stared at the thing, the lights of their headlamps centering on it, a yellow beam sometimes flickering over the sleeping man as one or another glanced at him.

'He made it, sure.'

'Sure enough.'

'What for?'

'Don't touch it.'

'I wasn't going to.'

Roused by their voices, the astronomer sat up. The yellow beams of the candles brought his face out white against the dark. He rubbed his eyes and greeted them.

'What would that be, lad?'

He looked troubled or confused when he saw the object of their curiosity. He put a hand on it protectively, yet he looked at it himself without seeming to recognize it for a while. At last he said, frowning and speaking in a whisper, 'It's a telescope.'

'What's that?'

'A device that makes distant things clear to the eye.'

'How come?' one of the miners asked, baffled. The astronomer answered him with growing assurance. 'By virtue of certain properties of light and lenses. The eye is a delicate instrument, but it is blind to half the universe – far more than half. The night sky is black, we say: between the stars is void and darkness. But turn the telescope-eye on that space between the stars, and lo, the stars! Stars too faint and far for the eye alone to see, rank behind rank, glory beyond glory, out to the

uttermost boundaries of the universe. Beyond all imagination, in the outer darkness, there is light: a great glory of sunlight. I have seen it. I have seen it, night after night, and mapped the stars, the beacons of God on the shores of the darkness. And here too there is light! There is no place bereft of the light, the comfort and radiance of the creator spirit. There is no place that is outcast, outlawed, forsaken. There is no place left dark. Where the eyes of God have seen, there light is. We must go farther, we must look farther! There is light if we will see it. Not with eyes alone, but with the skill of the hands and the knowledge of the mind and the heart's faith is the unseen revealed, and the hidden made plain. And all the dark earth shines like a sleeping star.'

He spoke with that authority which the miners knew belonged by rights to the priests, to the great words priests spoke in the echoing churches. It did not belong here, in the hole where they grubbed their living, in the words of a crazy fugitive. Later on, one talking to another, they shook their heads, or tapped them. Per said, 'The madness is growing in him,' and Hanno said, 'Poor soul, poor soul!' Yet there was not one of them who did not, also, believe what the astronomer had told them.

'Show me,' said old Bran, finding Guennar alone in a deep eastern drift, busy with his intricate device. It was Bran who had first followed Guennar, and brought him food, and led him back to the others.

The astronomer willingly stood aside and showed Bran how to hold the device pointing downward at the tunnel floor, and how to aim and focus it, and tried to describe its function and what Bran might see: all hesitantly, since he was not used to explaining to the ignorant, but without impatience when Bran did not understand.

'I don't see nothing but the ground,' the old man said after a long and solemn observation with the instrument. 'And the little dust and pebbles on it.'

'The lamp blinds your eyes, perhaps,' the astronomer said

with humility. 'It is better to look without light. I can do it because I have done it for so long. It is all practice – like placing the gads, which you always do right, and I always do wrong.'

'Aye. Maybe. Tell me what you see—' Bran hesitated. He had not long ago realized who Guennar must be. Knowing him to be a heretic made no difference but knowing him to be a learned man made it hard to call him 'mate' or 'lad'. And yet here, and after all this time, he could not call him Master. There were times when, for all his mildness, the fugitive spoke with great words, gripping one's soul, times when it would have been easy to call him Master. But it would have frightened him.

The astronomer put his hand on the frame of his mechanism and replied in a soft voice, 'There are . . . constellations.'

'What's that, constellations?'

The astronomer looked at Bran as if from a great way off, and said presently, 'The Wain, the Scorpion, the Sickle by the Milky Way in summer, those are constellations. Patterns of stars, gatherings of stars, parenthoods, semblances . . .'

'And you see those here, with this?'

Still looking at him through the weak lamplight with clear brooding eyes, the astronomer nodded, and did not speak, but pointed downward, at the rock on which they stood, the hewn floor of the mine.

'What are they like?' Bran's voice was hushed.

'I have only glimpsed them. Only for a moment. I have not learned the skill; it is a somewhat different skill . . . But they are there, Bran.'

Often now he was not in the stope where they worked, when they came to work, and did not join them even for their meal, though they always left him a share of food. He knew the ways of the mine now better than any of them, even Bran, not only the 'living' mine but the 'dead' one, the abandoned workings and exploratory tunnels that ran eastward, ever deeper, towards the caves. There he was most often; and they did not follow him.

When he did appear amongst them and they talked with him, they were more timid with him, and did not laugh.

One night as they were all going back with the last cartload to the main shaft, he came to meet them, stepping suddenly out of a crosscut to their right. As always he wore his ragged sheepskin coat, black with the clay and dirt of the tunnels. His fair hair had gone grey. His eyes were clear. 'Bran,' he said, 'come, I can show you now.'

'Show me what?'

'The stars. The stars beneath the rock. There's a great constellation in the stope on the old fourth level, where the white granite cuts down through the black.'

'I know the place.'

'It's there: underfoot, by that wall of white rock. A great shining and assembly of stars. Their radiance beats up through the darkness. They are like the faces of dancers, the eyes of angels. Come and see them, Bran!'

The miners stood there, Per and Hanno with backs braced to hold the cart from rolling: stooped men with tired, dirty faces and big hands bent and hardened by the grip of shovel and pick and sledge. They were embarrassed, compassionate, impatient.

'We're just quitting. Off home to supper. Tomorrow,' Bran said.

The astronomer looked from one face to another and said nothing.

Hanno said in his hoarse gentle voice, 'Come up with us, for this once, lad. It's dark night out, and likely raining; it's November now; no soul will see you if you come and sit at my hearth, for once, and eat hot food, and sleep beneath a roof and not under the heavy earth all by yourself alone!'

Guennar stepped back. It was as if a light went out, as his face went into shadow. 'No,' he said. 'They will burn out my eyes.'

'Leave him be,' said Per, and set the heavy ore-cart moving towards the shaft.

'Look where I told you,' Guennar said to Bran. 'The mine is not dead. Look with your own eyes.'

'Aye. I'll come with you and see. Good night!'

'Good night,' said the astronomer, and turned back to the side-tunnel as they went on. He carried no lamp or candle; they saw him one moment, darkness the next.

In the morning he was not there to meet them. He did not come.

Bran and Hanno sought him, idly at first, then for one whole day. They went as far down as they dared, and came at last to the entrance of the caves, and entered, calling sometimes, though in the great caverns even they, miners all their lives, dared not call aloud because of the terror of the endless echoes in the dark.

'He has gone down,' Bran said. 'Down farther. That's what he said. Go farther, you must go farther, to find the light.'

'There is no light,' Hanno whispered. 'There was never light here. Not since the world's creation.'

But Bran was an obstinate old man, with a literal and credulous mind; and Per listened to him. One day the two went to the place the astronomer had spoken of, where a great vein of hard light granite that cut down through the darker rock had been left untouched, fifty years ago, as barren stone. They retimbered the roof of the old stope where the supports had weakened, and began to dig, not into the white rock but down, beside it; the astronomer had left a mark there, a kind of chart or symbol drawn with candle-black on the stone floor. They came on silver ore a foot down, beneath the shell of quartz; and under that – all eight of them working now – the striking picks laid bare the raw silver, the veins and branches and knots and nodes shining among broken crystals in the shattered rock, like stars and gatherings of stars, depth below depth without end, the light.

THE FIELD OF VISION

*I hardly know what to say about 'The Field of Vision'; it is a
sort of sublimated temper tantrum. An indignant Letter to the
Editor. A raspberry.*

*Shelley was kicked out of Oxford – I think the story is un-
authenticated, but who cares – because he painted a sign on the
end wall of a dead-end alley:* THIS WAY TO HEAVEN. *I feel that
every now and then his sign needs repainting.*

I saw Eternity the other night
Like a great Ring of pure and endless light . . .
 —Henry Vaughan, 1621–1695

Reports from Psyche XIV came in regularly, all routine, until
just before their return window opened. Then all at once Com-
mander Rogers radioed that they had left surface, had rejoined
the ship, and were commencing departure procedures – 82
hours 18 minutes early. Houston of course demanded explana-
tions, but Psyche's answers were erratic. The 220-second
answer lag didn't help. Psyche kept breaking contact. Once
Rogers said, 'We have got to bring her home now if we're going
to do it at all,' apparently in answer to Houston's questions, but
the next thing was Hughes asking for a reading, and then some-
thing about a dosage. The sun was noisy and reception was very
bad. The voice transmission ceased without sign-off.

The automatic information feed from the ship continued.
Departure was normal. Normal, reports came in during the
twenty-six days of flight which the astronauts spent in drugged

sleep on HKL and I.V. hookups. There was no medical moni-
tor on Psyche missions. The only link with the crew was voice
contact. When they did not call in on Day 2, the long tension at
Houston tightened to despair.

The onboard automatics, directed by the ground crew, had
just about established Psyche's re-entry course when the dead
speakers suddenly said in Hughes's voice, 'Houston, can you
give me readings. Optical interference here.' They tried to
direct him, but the one attempt he made at a manual correction
was disastrous, and took ground control five hours to compen-
sate. They told him hands off, they'd bring in the ship. Almost
immediately after that they lost voice contact again.

The great pale parachutes opened above the grey Pacific,
roses slowly falling out of heaven. The speed-burnt ship
screamed steam, plunging; popped back up and rocked, quiet,
on the long deep swells. Ground control had done a beautiful
job. She was down within a half-kilo of the *California*. Heli-
copters hovered, rafts assembled, the ship was stabilized, the
hatch was opened. Nobody scrambled out.

They went in and brought them out.

Commander Rogers was in his flight seat, still strapped
down and plugged into the HKL and I.V.s. He had been dead
about ten days, and it was clear why the others had not opened
his suit.

Captain Temski seemed physically unhurt, but dazed and
bewildered. He did not speak, or respond to instructions. They
had to manhandle him to haul him out of the ship, though he
put up no active resistance.

Dr Hughes was in a state of collapse, but fully conscious; he
appeared to be blind.

'Please . . .'
'Can you see anything?'
'Yes! Please let me have the blindfold.'
'Do you see this light I'm showing? What color is it, Dr
Hughes?'

'All colors, white, it's too bright.'

'Will you point towards it, please?'

'It's everywhere. It's too bright.'

'The room's quite dark, Dr Hughes. Now, will you open your eyes again, please.'

'It isn't dark.'

'Mmmh. Possible supersensitivity here. All right now, how about that? Dark enough for you?'

'Make it dark!'

'No, keep your hands down, please. Take it easy. All right, we'll put the compresses back on.'

The struggling man relaxed as soon as his eyes were covered, and lay still, breathing hard. His narrow face, framed in a month's growth of dark beard, was oiled with sweat. 'I'm sorry,' he said.

'We'll try again later on when you've rested.'

'Will you open your eyes, please. The room's quite dark.'

'Why do you tell me that when it's *not* dark?'

'Dr Hughes, I can hardly make out your face; I've got the faintest red illumination on my scope – nothing else. Can you see me?'

'No! I can't see for the light!'

The doctor increased the illumination until he could see Hughes's face, the clenched jaw, the open, dazzled, frightened eyes.

'There, does that make it any darker?' he asked with the sarcasm of helplessness.

'No!' Hughes shut his eyes; he had gone dead white. 'Get dizzy,' he muttered, 'the whirling,' then he gasped for breath and began to vomit.

Hughes was unmarried and had no immediate kin. His closest friend was known to be Bernard Decelis. They had trained together; Decelis had been specialist on Psyche XII, the mission that had discovered the City of Mars, as Hughes

was on XIV. They flew Decelis to the debriefing station in
Pasadena and instructed him to go in and talk with his friend.
The conversation was of course recorded.

D. *Hullo, Gerry. Decelis.*

H. *Barnie?*

D. *How you doing?*

H. *Fine. You been OK?*

D. *Sure. No picnic, was it?*

H. *How's Gloria?*

D. *Fine, just fine.*

H. *She got past 'Aunt Rhody' yet?*

D. *[laughs] Oh, Christ, yeah. She can play 'Greensleeves' now.
At least she calls it 'Greensleeves'.*

H. *What have they got you in this dump for?*

D. *To see you.*

H. *Wish I could return the compliment.*

D. *You will. Listen. I've been assured by three different
oculists, or whatever the hell they are, opthamollywhoggers,
eye-doctors here, that there is absolutely nothing wrong with
your eyes. Three opthamacadamizers and a neurologist, in
fact. It's a sort of chorus they have. But they sure as hell
seem sure of it.*

H. *So what's wrong is my brain, evidently.*

D. *In the sense of a crossed connection, maybe.*

H. *What about Joe Temski?*

D. *I don't know. Haven't seen him.*

H. *What did they tell you about him?*

D. *They didn't have a chorus line worked out for him. Just
said he's inclined to be withdrawn.*

H. *Withdrawn! Jesus, I'll say so. Like a rock is withdrawn.*

D. *Temski? That joker?*

H. *It started with him.*

D. *What did?*

H. *At the site. He stopped answering.*

D. *What happened?*

H. Just that. He stopped answering. Stopped talking. Stopped noticing. Dwight thought it was cafard. Is that what they're still calling it?

D. It's mentioned as one possibility. Was there anything special happened, there at the site?

H. We found the room.

D. The room, yeah. That all came back on your reports. I've seen them, and some of the holos you brought back with you. Fantastic. What the hell is it, Gerry?

H. I don't know.

D. Is it a construct?

H. I don't know. What's the whole City?

D. It was built, made; it must have been.

H. How do you know, how can you tell, when you don't know what made it? Is a seashell 'made'? If you didn't know, if you didn't have any background and couldn't assume any likeness, and you looked at a seashell and a ceramic ashtray, could you tell, could you say which was 'made'? And what for? What does it mean? Or what about a ceramic seashell? Or a paperwasp's nest? Or a geode?

D. Yeah, OK. But what about those things, that . . . arrangement that you call 'pigeonholes' in the reports? I saw the holos. What did you make of them?

H. What did you make of them?

D. I don't know. They're weird. I thought of running the spatial arrangements through a computer, looking for meaningful pattern . . . You don't think much of that.

H. No. Fine. Only what are you going to program for 'meaning'?

D. Mathematical relationships. Any kind of geometrical pattern, regularity, code. I don't know. What was the place like, Gerry?

H. I don't know.

D. You were in there a lot?

H. All the time, after we found it.

D. *That's where you noticed this kind of eye trouble you've got? How did it start?*

H. *Things going out of focus. Like eye strain. It was worse outside the room. Came on over several days. I could still make things out all right when we were taking the ML up to the ship. But getting worse. There'd be these flashes of light, left my depth perception all screwed up, I'd get dizzy. Dwight and I set up the course, one or the other of us was functioning most of the time. But he was getting kind of wild. Didn't want to use the radio, wouldn't touch the onboard computer.*

D. *What was . . . wrong with him?*

H. *I don't know. When I told him about my eyes he said he'd been having something like shaking fits. I said we'd better get the hell up to the ship while we could. He said OK, because Joe was really beginning to not function. Before we even launched he started having some kind of seizures, like epilepsy – Dwight, I mean. When he came out of one he was shaky, but he seemed rational. He took us up OK, but as soon as we docked in he went into another fit, and they kept getting longer. He started hallucinating in between them. I gave him some tranquillizers and strapped him in; it was wearing him out. When I took the sleep, I don't know, he could have been dead already then.*

D. *No, he died in the sleep. About ten days out from Earth.*

H. *They didn't tell me that.*

D. *There wasn't anything you could have done, Gerry.*

H. *I don't know. Those attacks he had, they were like overloads. Like all his fuses blew. Burned him out. He talked, while he was in them. Sort of in bursts, like barking – as if he was trying to say a whole sentence at once. Epileptics don't talk, do they, when they're having a seizure?*

D. *I don't know. Epilepsy's so well controlled now you don't hear much about it. They catch the tendency, and cure it first. If Rogers had had the tendency . . .*

H. *Yeah. He never would have been in the program. Christ,
he'd had six months in space.*

D. *What had you had – six days?*

H. *Like you. One Moon hop.*

D. *It isn't that, then. Do you think . . .*

H. *What?*

D. *Some kind of virus?*

H. *Space plague? Martian fever? Mysterious ancient spores
madden astronauts?*

D. *All right, it sounds dumb. But look, the room had been
sealed. And it does sound like all of you—*

H. *Dwight gets a cortical overcharge, Joe goes catatonic, I
start seeing things. What's the connection?*

D. *Nervous system.*

H. *Why different symptoms in each of us?*

D. *Well, drugs affect people differently—*

H. *Do you think we found some kind of God damned Martian
psychogenic mushrooms in there? There isn't anything there,
it's dead, like all the rest of Mars. You know, you've been
there! There aren't any God damned germs or viruses,
there's no life there, no life.*

D. *But there may have been—*

H. *What makes you think so?*

D. *The room you found. The City we found.*

H. *City! For Christ's sake, Barnie, you talk like some damned
pop journalist, you know damned well the whole thing is a
set of mud concretions for all we can tell. There's no way to
tell. It's too old, conditions are too different, we have no
context. We don't understand, we can't understand, it's
something the human mind is outside of. Cities, rooms, all
that – we're just analogizing, trying to make sense in our
terms. But it's not in our terms. There is no sense. I can see
that now. That's the only thing I can see!*

D. *See what, Gerry?*

H. *What I see when I open my eyes!*

D. *What?*

H. Everything that isn't there and doesn't make sense. Oh—I—
D. Here, come on. Take it easy. Look, it'll be OK. It's going to
 be OK, Gerry, you'll be OK.
H. [unclear] light, and the [unclear] try to see what I touch
 and I can't, I don't understand and I can't [unclear]
D. Hang on. I'm right here. Take it easy, old man.

Hughes, who had entered the space program from as-
trophysics, came with a very good record, in fact a brilliant one.
This troubled many of his military superiors, to whom high
intelligence was a code word for instability and insub-
ordination. His performance had been solid and his behavior
irreproachable; but now it was frequently recalled that he was,
after all, an intellectual.

Temski was harder to explain. He was a crack test pilot, an
Air Force captain, and a baseball fan, but now his behavior was
even more aberrant than Hughes's.

All Temski did was sit. He was capable of looking after
himself, and did so. That is, when he was hungry and food was
present, he ate some with his fingers; when he had to relieve
himself, he went to a corner and did so; when he was sleepy, he
lay down on the floor and slept. The rest of the time he sat. He
was in good physical condition and quite calm. Nothing said to
him produced the slightest reaction, nor did he take any interest
in anything that went on. His wife was brought in to see him in
hopes of producing a response. She was taken away weeping
after five minutes.

Since Temski wouldn't respond, and Rogers, being dead,
couldn't respond, it was quite natural to look upon Hughes as
being, somehow, responsible.

There was nothing wrong with him except a case of some-
thing like hysterical blindness, so it was to be expected that he
should answer questions rationally and explain precisely what
had happened. This, however, he could not, or would not, do.

A psychiatric consultant was brought in, a distinguished
New York doctor called Shapir. He was requested to work with

both Temski and Hughes. It was of course unthinkable to admit that the mission had been a failure (the word 'disaster' was not even mentioned), but a couple of rumors had leaked out to the press despite all security precautions. Irresponsible journalists demanded to know why the crew of Psyche XIV was being held incommunicado, and claimed the 'right' of the American people to 'know', etc. It had been necessary to issue a statement concerning a new health test being run on astronauts who had spent over fifteen days in space, due to Commander Rogers's unexpected and tragic death from heart failure, and to have a whole new series of articles written for the papers concerning plans for a 'Little America' dome city on Mars, to maintain a positive attitude in the public. The real people of course knew that the rest of the Psyche program was in jeopardy; and they instructed Dr Shapir to diagnose and cure the astronauts with all deliberate speed.

Shapir talked with Hughes for half an hour about the food in the hospital, Cal Tech, and the latest Chinese report on their Alpha Centauri probe, all very relaxed and trivial. Then he said, 'What is it you see, when you open your eyes?'

Hughes, who was up and dressed now, sat silent for a while. Opaque goggles covered his eyes entirely, giving him the arrogant, staring look of people who affect dark glasses. 'Nobody's asked that,' he said.

'Didn't the oculists?'

'Yes, I guess Kray did. Early on. Before they decided I was a mental case.'

'What did you tell him?'

'It's hard to describe. The point is, it's indescribable. At first it was things going out of focus, going transparent, going away. Then the light. Too much light. Like overexposing a film, bleaching everything out. But with that, a kind of whirling. Changing positions and relationships, changing perspectives, constant transformation. It made me get dizzy. My eyes kept sending signals to my inner ears, I guess. Like that inner-ear

disease, only in reverse. Doesn't it foul up your spatial orientation?'

'Ménière's syndrome, I think it's called, yes, it does. Especially on stairs and slopes.'

'It's as if I was looking from a great height, or . . . up at a great height . . .'

'Heights ever worry you?'

'Hell no. They don't even mean anything to me. What's up and down, in space? No, see, I'm not giving you the picture. There is no picture. I've been trying to look more, to learn to . . . how to see . . . it's not much good.'

There was a pause. 'That takes courage,' said Shapir.

'What do you mean?' the astronaut said sharply.

'Well . . . To have the sensory input which is most important to the conscious mind – sight – reporting non-existent and incomprehensible things, in flagrant contradiction with all other sensory input – your touch, your hearing, your sense of balance, and so on – to have that going on, every time you try to open your eyes, and not only to live with it but to attempt to investigate it . . . It doesn't sound easy.'

'So mostly I keep my eyes shut,' Hughes said, dour. 'Like a damned see-no-evil monkey.'

'When you do have your eyes open, and you look towards some object you know is there – your own hand, for instance – what do you see?'

' "A blooming, buzzing confusion." '

'William James,' Shapir said with satisfaction. 'What was he talking about – how a baby perceives the world, eh?' He had a pleasant voice with a mild, glancing quality to it, non-percussive; one could not imagine him scolding or yelling. He nodded several times, thinking out the implications of what Hughes had said. 'To learn how to see, you said. To learn. That's how you feel about it?'

Hughes hesitated, then said with a sudden, marked increase of trust, 'I have to. What else can I do? Apparently I'm never

going to be able to – to see the way I used to, the way other people do, again. But I still do *see*. Only I don't understand what I see, it doesn't make sense. There are no outlines, no distinctions, even between nearer and farther. There *is* something there – only I can't say that, because there aren't any *things*. No forms. Instead of forms, I see transformations – transfigurations. Does that make any sense at all?'

'I think it does,' Shapir said, 'only it's enormously difficult to put a direct experience into words. And when the experience is new, unique, overwhelming . . .'

'And irrational. That's it.' Hughes spoke now with real gratitude. 'If only I could show it to you,' he said wistfully.

The two astronauts were being kept on the tenth floor of a big military hospital in Maryland now. They were not permitted to leave that floor, and anyone who visited it still spent ten days in quarantine before he rejoined the outer world: the Martian plague theory was currently on top. At Shapir's insistence, Hughes was allowed to go up to the roof garden of the hospital (after which the elevator was elaborately sterilized and roped off for three days).

They demanded that Hughes wear a surgical mask; and Shapir had asked him not to wear his goggles. Docile, he went up the elevator with his mouth and nose covered, his eyes uncovered, but tightly shut.

The change from the dusk of the elevator to the hot smoggy sunlight of July on the open roof did not, as far as Shapir could see, affect those shut eyes. Hughes did not screw them tighter against the flooding light, though he raised his face to it as if he felt the heat pleasant on his skin, and took a deep breath through the binding gauze.

'I haven't been outside since March,' he said.

It was true, of course. He had been in a spacesuit or in a hospital room, breathing canned or conditioned air.

'Have you got your compass bearings?' Shapir asked.

'Not the faintest. It makes me feel blinder, being outdoors. Afraid to walk off the edge.' Hughes had refused assistance

coming through the corridors and in the elevator, feeling his way adeptly with his hands, and now despite his joke about falling off he began to explore the roof garden. He was exhilarated: an active man released from long confinement. Shapir watched him, brooding. The low furniture was a hazard to him but he learned at once how to feel for it; he had tactile intelligence; there was grace in his movements, even as he blundered in blindness.

'Will you open your eyes?' Shapir said in his glancing, reluctant voice.

Hughes stopped. 'All right,' he said; but he turned towards Shapir, and his right hand came up gropingly. Shapir came forward and let that hand take his arm.

The grip of it tightened, as Hughes opened his eyes. Then Hughes let go, and took a step away, stretching out both his arms. A cry broke from him. He reached forward and upward, his head back, his eyes wide open, staring at the empty sky. 'Oh, my God!' he whispered, and dropped, like a man hit by a sledgehammer.

Psychiatric counselling session, 18th July. S. Shapir, Geraint Hughes.

S. Hello. Sidney . . . I won't stay long. Listen, that wasn't such a bright idea of mine. The roof. I'm sorry. I had no idea. But no right, either . . . Would you rather I left?

H. No.

S. All right . . . I'm getting stir-crazy myself. Need a good walk. I walk a good deal, usually. About two miles to my office and the same back. Then I add detours. Whatever they say, New York is a beautiful town to walk in. If you know how to pick your route. Listen, I have a queer story about Joe Temski. Not a story, just a queer fact, actually. Did you know that they have written on his record that he is 'functionally deaf'?

H. Deaf?

S. Yes, deaf. Well, you know, I began to wonder. I go in and

talk to Joe, you know, touch him, try to make eye contact,
any kind of contact, to get through. No go. I've had patients
tell me in so many words, 'I can't hear you.' A metaphor. But
what if it isn't a metaphor? It happens sometimes with little
kids, they're called retarded and it turns out they've got
thirty, sixty, eighty percent hearing dysfunction. Well,
maybe Joe really can't hear me. Just like you can't see me.

H. [pause of forty seconds] Do you mean he's hearing things?
Listening?

S. It's possible.

H. [pause of twenty seconds] You can't shut your ears.

S. That's what I thought, too. It could be rough, couldn't it?
Well, what I thought was, what about trying to shut them for
him? Put earplugs in his ears.

H. He still wouldn't be able to hear you.

S. No, but he wouldn't be distracted. If you had to watch your
light show all the time, you wouldn't be able to pay much
attention to me or anything else, right? Maybe it's like that
with Joe. Maybe there's this noise drowning out everything
else for him.

H. [pause of twenty seconds] It would be more than noise.

S. I don't suppose you want to talk about . . . on the roof . . .
No, all right.

H. You'd like to know what I saw, wouldn't you?

S. Sure I would. But in your own time.

H. Yeah, I've got so much else to do here besides talk to you.
All the books I can read and the beautiful women I can look
at. You know damned well I'll tell you eventually, because I
haven't got anybody else to talk to.

S. Oh, hell, Geraint. [pause of ten seconds]

H. Shit. I'm sorry, Sidney. If I didn't have you to talk to, I'd
have cracked completely. I know that. You're very patient
with me.

S. Whatever you saw, up there, disturbs you. That's one reason
why I want to know what it was. But what the hell, if you can
handle it alone, do. That's the idea, after all. My curiosity is

my problem, not yours! Listen. Let's forget talking. Let me
read you this article in Science. *Your Colonel Wood gave it*
to me, said you might be interested. I was. It's on what they
found inside the Argentinian meteorite. The authors are
suggesting we go comb the Meteor Belt for remnants of a
trans-stellar fleet that came to grief in our solar system about
six hundred million years ago. They would have landed on
Mars first, of course. Are these guys nuts?
H. *I don't know. Read the article.*

Temski slept heavily, and it was easy for Shapir to insert
ordinary wax plugs like those insomniacs use into his ears while
he was asleep. When Temski woke he did nothing unusual at
first. He sat up, yawned, stretched, scratched, looked lazily
around to see if anything to eat was handy, in that serene way
which Shapir privately felt was altogether unlike any psychotic
behavior he had ever seen, and in fact unlike any human be-
havior he had ever seen. Temski reminded him of a healthy,
poised, contented, tame animal. Not a chimpanzee; something
milder, more contemplative, an orang, maybe.

But the orang began to feel uncomfortable.

Temski looked around, left and right, nervous. Perhaps he
was not looking but moving his head trying to find the vanished
sounds. The lost chord, Shapir thought. Temski grew more and
more disturbed and alert. He got up, still turning his head
restlessly. He looked across the room. For the first time in
seventeen days of daily contact, he saw Shapir.

His handsome face was now contorted with anxiety or be-
wilderment.

'Where,' he said, 'where—'

His hands, groping at his ears to find the cause of silence,
found the earplugs and removed one. That was enough. 'Ah,' he
said, and stood still. His eyes were still directed towards
Shapir, but he did not see him. His face relaxed.

Later attempts were more successful. Though bewildered at
first, Temski was cooperative while artificially deafened, and

responded readily to Shapir's attempts to communicate with him by touch, by sign, and finally by writing. After the fifth such session, Temski consented to longer sessions involving the use of a drug which would deaden his auditory nerve endings for about five hours at a time.

During the second of these long periods he asked to see Hughes. Shapir had already been instructed to let the two astronauts talk together if possible; there was a feeling that this might elicit more information, if they talked freely together. It was necessary for Hughes to write, since Temski was artificially deafened; as he knew touch typing he carried on his part of the dialogue on a portable typewriter. Not all the material found in the wastebasket, however, could be successfully collated in to the tape of Temski's spoken conversation. The two men mostly discussed the return journey and Commander Rogers's illness and death, which Temski could not recall; Hughes described all this as he had done before without new information. They did not talk about the 'room' (Site D) or their respective disabilities, except as follows:

T. It's not inside, is it?
H. If it was, earplugs wd improve yr reception.
T. It's real, then.
H. Hell yes.
T. See, when they first stuck those plugs in my ears, when I woke up and there was this silence, I was really spooked. It took me a long time to come back from where I'd been. And I didn't much want to come back. But when Shapir began telling me how long it had been, and I realized this was Earth, you know, that's what spooked me – I thought, maybe all this has been some sort of, like, hallucination. You know, Jesus, have I been off my chump? That scared me. Like I was two different people. But I began to put it together, to see that it wasn't a split, but a . . .
H. Change.

T. *Exactly, it changed me, it had changed me. It's real. Because when I can hear, that's what I hear. And when you can see, that's what you see. Right? In other words, it is real. We have to be artificially blinded and made deaf to not hear it and see it. That's it, isn't it?*

[*Hughes's typed responses for the following section were not identifiable in the wastebasket material.*]

H. . . .

T. *Oh, no. Beautiful. It took me a long time, at least I know now it was a long time, to begin to get it. At first it didn't make any sense, Jesus, it scared the balls off me at first. You or Dwight would say something, and there'd be this kind of chords all around your voice, like rainbows around a prism so you can't even see the prism – yeah, that's what it's like for you, isn't it? It's the same, only this is with hearing, it's like everything turns into this music, only it isn't music, it's . . . At first like I said I didn't know how to hear it. I thought it was something wrong with my suit radio! Jesus!* [*laughs*] *I couldn't follow the patterns, you know, the modulations, like, the transformations. It was all so different. But you learn. The more you listen the more you hear. I wish you could hear it. You know, you tell me it's two months since we left Mars, and so on, and shit, I believe you, but it doesn't matter. It really doesn't matter – does it, Gerry?*

H. . . .

T. *I wish I could see it, the way you do. It must be tremendous. But I'll tell you, I'm glad they pull me out of it like this, every day now. I think it's meant to be that way. I was kind of, I don't know, swamped, overwhelmed, it's too much. We're not built right, not quite strong enough, maybe. At least at first. Can't take it all at once. What I'd like to try to do while I'm out of touch is try to write some of it down.*

H. . . .

T. *No, I don't. But it wouldn't have to be music. See, it isn't music, that's just like a way of describing it because it's beautiful. I think I could get it into words just as well.*

Maybe better. To say what it means.
H. ...
T. *Afraid of what?*

Bernard Decelis and his wife called Hughes every couple of days on the telephone, though they were prevented by the quarantine from coming to see him. On the 27th of July Hughes and Decelis had a significant conversation concerning the so-called room, site D of the Psyche XIV survey. Decelis said, 'If I don't get on the Sixteen team and *see* that damned place, I'll flip.'

'Seeing is believing,' Hughes remarked. He was not as excitable as he had been earlier, tending to be terse and rather bitter.

'Listen, Terry. Was there ever machinery in those pigeon-holes?'

'No.'

'Hah! There's a definite answer! I thought you wouldn't assert anything about Site D except its incomprehensibility to the human mind. You softening up?'

'No. Learning.'

'Learning what?'

'How to see.'

After a pause Decelis asked cautiously, 'See what?'

'Site D. Since it's all I can see.'

'You mean, that's what you – when your eyes are open—'

'No.' Hughes spoke wearily and with reluctance. 'It's more complex than that. I don't see Site D. I see ... the world in the light cast by Site D ... A new light. The man you ought to ask is Joe Temski. Or, listen, did you ever run the pigeonholes through Algie, like you said?'

'I had trouble setting up the program.'

'I'll bet you did,' Hughes said with a short laugh. 'Send the stuff on up here. I'll set it up. Blindfolded.'

Temski came into Hughes's room, radiant. 'Gerry,' he said, 'I've got it.'

'Got what?'

'I've got it together. I heard you. No, I wasn't lip-reading. Say something with your back turned. Go on!'

'Ptomaine poisoning.'

' "Ptomaine poisoning." —OK? See, I'm hearing you. But I haven't lost the music. I've got it all together!'

Blue-eyed and fair, Temski was ordinarily a handsome man; now he was magnificent. Hughes could not see him (though the spy camera in the ventilator grille could and did), but he heard the vibration of his voice, and was moved, and frightened.

'Take off your blinkers, Gerry,' the gentle, vibrant voice said.

Hughes shook his head.

'You can't sit in the dark inside yourself forever. Come out. You can't choose blindness, Gerry.'

'Why can't I?'

'Not after you've seen the light.'

'What light?'

'The light, the word, the truth we have been taught to perceive and to know,' Temski said, with the gentleness of utter certainty, and a warmth in his voice, a warmth like sunlight.

'Get out,' Hughes said. 'Get out, Temski!'

Twelve weeks had passed since Psyche XIV splashdown. Nobody on the debriefing staff had come down with any symptoms more alarming than boredom. Hughes was no worse, and Temski was now completely recovered. It could be safely assumed that whatever had affected the crew of Psyche XIV, it had not been an infection vectored by a virus, spore, bacterium, or other physical agent. The hypothesis accepted tentatively and with various reservations by the majority, including Dr Shapir, was that something in the arrangement of the elements constituting the 'room', Site D, had, during their prolonged and intense study of the site, caused a degree of brain-wave disruption in all three men, analogous to the brain-function disturbance caused by strobe lights at certain frequencies, etc. Precisely what elements of the 'room' were involved was not

yet known, though the holographs were being examined intensively by experts. Psyche XV was to make a still more thorough investigation of the site, taking due precautions to protect and monitor the astronauts.

These suspect elements of Site D were so numerous and so intricately interrelated that it was very hard for a single mind to attempt to arrange or order them. Some Martianologists were sure the peculiar properties of the 'room' were only a geological accident, and that all the 'room' had to 'tell' us was the kind of information furnished so concisely and beautifully by the strata of rocks, the rings of a tree, the lines of a spectrum. Others were as convinced that intelligent beings had built the City, and that in studying it we might learn something of their nature and the way their minds worked – those unimaginable minds of six hundred million years ago (for the radioactive-decay dating of the site was absolutely definite now). The job of doing so, however, was daunting. T. A. Newman of the Smithsonian Institution put it well: 'Archaeologists are used to getting a lot of information out of very simple things – potsherds, bits of flint, a wall here, a grave there. But what if all we had of an ancient civilization was a very complicated thing, complicated in more than a technological sense – let's say, one copy of Shakespeare's *Hamlet*. Now let's assume that the archaeologists who find this copy of *Hamlet* are not humanoid, don't have books, don't have plays, don't speak, write, or think at all as we do. What are they going to make of that little physical artifact, the evident complexity and purposefulness of it, the repetition of certain elements and the non-repetition of others, the semi-regularity of line lengths, and so on? How are they going to read *Hamlet*?'

To those who accepted the '*Hamlet* theory', the obvious first step was to employ computers, and a number of them had been set to work analyzing the various elements of Site D: the spacing, size, depth, and configurations of the 'pigeonholes', the proportions of the first, middle, and third 'subchambers', the extraordinary acoustical properties of the 'room' as a whole,

and so on. None of these programs had as yet produced any sure evidence of conscious planning or rational pattern; none, that is, except the program set up by Decelis and Hughes on NASA's new Algebraic V, which had certainly got results, though they could not be called rational. Indeed, that print-out had given a shudder to the NASA brass, and a good laugh to those few scientists to whom Decelis had shown it before it was suppressed as being probably a fraud and certainly an embarrassment. The entire print-out read as follows:

```
RUN
PIGEONHOLES SITE D MARS SECTOR NINE
DECELIS  HUGHES

GOD

GOOD GOD GOD GOOD YOU ARE GOD

RESET

RESET TOTALITY COMPREHENSION NONSENSE
PERCEIVE NONSENSE NO SENSE REAL GOOD GOD

PERCEIVE  RECEIVE  DIRECTIONS  DIRECTION

PROCEED  INFORM  UNINFORMED

GOD GOD GOD GOD GOD GOD

END RUN
```

Shapir came in to find Hughes lying on his bed, as he now did most of the time, wearing his black goggles. He looked white and ill.

'I think you've been overdoing it.'

Hughes did not answer.

Shapir sat down. 'They're sending me back to New York,' he said presently.

Hughes did not answer.

'Temski's been released, you know. He's on his way to Florida now. With his wife. I can't find out what they plan for you. I asked . . .' After a long pause he completed the sentence. 'I asked for another two weeks here with you. No go.'

'It's all right,' Hughes said.

'I want to keep in touch with you, Geraint. Obviously we can't write letters. But there's the phone. And tapes; I'm leaving a casette recorder here with you. When you want to talk, please call me. If you can't get me, talk to the recorder. It's not the same, but—'

'You're a very good man, Sidney,' Hughes said gently. 'I wish . . .' After a minute he sat up. He reached up to his face and took off the black goggles. They fitted so closely around his eyes sockets that it took him a little while to get them off. When they were off he lowered his hands, and looked across the room, directly at Shapir. His eyes, the pupils enlarged by long privation of light, were almost as dark as the goggles.

'I see you,' he said. 'Hide and seek. I spy. You're It. Do you want to know what I see?'

'Yes,' Shapir said softly.

'A blot. A shadow. An incompleteness, a rudiment, an obstruction. Something completely unimportant. You see, it doesn't do any *good* to be a good man, even . . .'

'And when you look at yourself?'

'The same. Just the same. A hindrance, a triviality. A blot on the field of vision.'

'The field of vision. What is the field of vision?'

'What do you think?' Hughes said, very quietly and wearily. 'What is true vision of? Reality, of course. I have been reprogrammed to perceive reality, to see the truth. I see God.' He sank his face into his hands, covering his eyes. 'I was a thinking man,' he said. 'I tried to be a rational man. But what good's

reason, when you can *see* the truth? Seeing is believing . . .' He looked up again at Shapir, his dark eyes both piercing and unseeing. 'If you want a real explanation, go ask Joe Temski. He's keeping quiet now; he's biding his time. But he's the one who can tell you. And he will, when his time comes. He can translate what he hears – translate it into words. It's harder to do with visual perceptions. Mystics have always had trouble putting their visions into words; except the ones that got the Word, that heard the Voice. They usually got right up and acted, didn't they? Temski will act. But I will not. I refuse. I will not preach. I will not be a missionary.'

'A missionary?'

'Don't you see? Don't you see that's what the "room" is? A training center, a briefing room, a—'

'A religious center? A church?'

'Well, in a way. A place where you are taught to see God, and hear God, and know God. And love God. A conversion center. A place where you're converted! And then you want to go out and preach the knowledge of God to the others – to the heathen. Because now you know how blind they are, and how easy it is to see. No, not just a church; a mission. The Mission. And you learn the Mission, and you come out of it with the Mission. They weren't explorers. They were missionaries, bearing the truth, bringing it to the other races and the future races, all the poor damned heathens living in the outer darkness. They knew the answer, and they wanted us all to know the answer. Nothing else matters, once you've learned the answer. It doesn't matter if you're a good man or a bad one, if I'm an intelligent man or a fool. Nothing about us matters except that we are trivial vehicles of the great truth. The earth doesn't matter, the stars don't matter, death doesn't matter, nothing is anything. Only God is.'

'An alien god?'

'Not a god. God – the one true God, immanent in all things. Everywhere, forever. I have learned to see God. All I have to do is open my eyes, and I see the Face of God. And I'd give all

my life just to see one human face again, to see a tree, a chair – a plain wooden chair, ordinary— They can keep their God, they can keep their Light. I want the world back. I want questions, not the answer. I want my own life back, and my own death!'

On the recommendation of the Army psychiatrist who took over the case of Geraint Hughes after Shapir was dismissed, Hughes was moved to a military hospital for the insane. As he was generally a quiet and cooperative patient he was not kept under strict supervision, and after eleven months of confinement he unfortunately carried out a successful suicide attempt, slashing his wrists with a spoon-handle which he had stolen from the mess hall and sharpened by rubbing against the bed frame. It is an interesting fact that he killed himself on the day the Psyche XV Mission started back to Earth from Mars, bringing the documents and records which, as interpreted by the First Apostle, now form the first chapters of the Revelation of the Ancients, the sacred texts of the holy and universal Church of God, bringer of light to the heathen, sole vehicle of the One Eternal Truth.

O fools (said I) thus to prefer dark night
 Before true light . . .
But as I did their madness so discuss
 One whisper'd thus,
This Ring the Bride-groome did for none provide
 But for his bride.

DIRECTION OF THE ROAD

The tree stands just south of the McMinnville bypass on Oregon State Highway 18. It lost a major limb last year, but still looks grand. We drive past it several times a year, and it has never failed to uphold Relativity with dignity and the skill of long practice.

They did not use to be so demanding. They never hurried us into anything more than a gallop, and that was rare; most of the time it was just a jigjog foot-pace. And when one of them was on his own feet, it was a real pleasure to approach him. There was time to accomplish the entire act with style. There he'd be, working his legs and arms the way they do, usually looking at the road, but often aside at the fields, or straight at me: and I'd approach him steadily but quite slowly, growing larger all the time, synchronizing the rate of approach and the rate of growth perfectly, so that at the very moment that I'd finished enlarging from a tiny speck to my full size – sixty feet in those days – I was abreast of him and hung above him, loomed, towered, over-shadowed him. Yet he would show no fear. Not even the children were afraid of me, though often they kept their eyes on me as I passed by and started to diminish.

Sometimes on a hot afternoon one of the adults would stop me right there at our meeting-place, and lie down with his back against mine for an hour or more. I didn't mind in the least. I have an excellent hill, good sun, good wind, good view; why should I mind standing still for an hour or an afternoon? It's only a relative stillness, after all. One need only look at the sun

to realize how fast one is going; and then, one grows continually – especially in summer. In any case I was touched by the way they would entrust themselves to me, letting me lean against their little warm backs and falling sound asleep there between my feet. I liked them. They have seldom lent us Grace as do the birds; but I really preferred them to squirrels.

In those days the horses used to work for them, and that too was enjoyable from my point of view. I particularly liked the canter, and got quite proficient at it. The surging and rhythmical motion accompanied shrinking and growing with a swaying and swooping, almost an illusion of flight. The gallop was less pleasant. It was jerky, pounding: one felt tossed about like a sapling in a gale. And then, the slow approach and growth, the moment of looming-over, and the slow retreat and diminishing, all that was lost during the gallop. One had to hurl oneself into it, cloppety-cloppety-cloppety! and the man usually too busy riding, and the horse too busy running, even to look up. But then, it didn't happen often. A horse is mortal, after all, and like all the loose creatures grows tired easily; so they didn't tire their horses unless there was urgent need. And they seemed not to have so many urgent needs, in those days.

It's been a long time since I had a gallop and to tell the truth I shouldn't mind having one. There was something invigorating about it, after all.

I remember the first motorcar I saw. Like most of us, I took it for a mortal, some kind of loose creature new to me. I was a bit startled, for after a hundred and thirty-two years I thought I knew all the local fauna. But a new thing is always interesting, in its trivial fashion, so I observed this one with attention. I approached it at a fair speed, about the rate of a canter, but in a new gait, suitable to the ungainly looks of the thing: an uncomfortable, bouncing, rolling, choking, jerking gait. Within two minutes, before I'd grown a foot tall, I knew it was no mortal creature, bound or loose or free. It was a making, like the carts the horses got hitched to. I thought it so very ill-made that I didn't expect it to return, once it gasped over the West

Hill, and I heartily hoped it never would for I disliked that jerking bounce.

But the thing took to a regular schedule, and so, perforce, did I. Daily at four I had to approach it, twitching and stuttering out of the West, and enlarge, loom-over, and diminish. Then at five back I had to come, poppeting along like a young jack-rabbit for all my sixty feet jigging and jouncing out of the East, until at last I got clear out of sight of the wretched little monster and could relax and loosen my limbs to the evening wind. There were always two of them inside the machine: a young male holding the wheel, and behind him an old female wrapped in rugs, glowering. if they ever said anything to each other I never heard it. In those days I overheard a good many conversations on the road, but not from that machine. The top of it was open, but it made so much noise that it overrode all voices, even the voice of the song-sparrow I had with me that year. The noise was almost as vile as the jouncing.

I am of a family of rigid principle and considerable self-respect. The Quercian motto is 'Break but bend not', and I have always tried to uphold it. It was not only personal vanity, but family pride, you see, that was offended when I was forced to jounce and bounce in this fashion by a mere making.

The apple trees in the orchard at the foot of the hill did not seem to mind; but then, apples are tame. Their genes have been tampered with for centuries. Besides, they are herd creatures; no orchard tree can really form an opinion of its own.

I kept my own opinion to myself.

But I was very pleased when the motorcar ceased to plague us. All month went by without it, and all month I walked at men and trotted at horses most willingly, and even bobbed for a baby on its mother's arm, trying hard though unsuccessfully to keep in focus.

Next month, however – September it was, for the swallows had left a few days earlier – another of the machines appeared, a new one, suddenly dragging me and the road and our hill, the orchard, the fields, the farmhouse roof, all jigging and jouncing

and racketing along from East to West; I went faster than a gallop, faster than I had ever gone before. I had scarcely time to loom, before I had to shrink right down again.

And the next day there came a different one.

Yearly then, weekly, daily, they became commoner. They became a major feature of the local Order of Things. The road was dug up and re-metalled, widened, finished off very smooth and nasty, like a slug's trail, with no ruts, pools, rocks, flowers, or shadows on it. There used to be a lot of little loose creatures on the road, grasshoppers, ants, toads, mice, foxes, and so on, most of them too small to move for, since they couldn't really see one. Now the wise creatures took to avoiding the road, and the unwise ones got squashed. I have seen all too many rabbits die in that fashion, right at my feet. I am thankful that I am an oak, and that though I may be wind-broken or uprooted, hewn or sawn, at least I cannot, under any circumstances, be squashed.

With the presence of many motorcars on the road at once, a new level of skill was required of me. As a mere seedling, as soon as I got my head above the weeds, I had learned the basic trick of going two directions at once. I learned it without thinking about it, under the simple pressure of circumstances on the first occasion that I saw a walker in the East and a horseman facing him in the West. I had to go two directions at once, and I did so. It's something we trees master without real effort, I suppose. I was nervous, but I succeeded in passing the rider and then shrinking away from him while at the same time I was still jigjogging towards the walker, and indeed passed him (no looming, back in those days!) only when I had got quite out of sight of the rider. I was proud of myself, being very young, that first time I did it; but it sounds more difficult than it really is. Since those days of course I had done it innumerable times, and thought nothing about it; I could do it in my sleep. But have you ever considered the feat accomplished, the skill involved, when a tree enlarges, simultaneously yet at slightly different rates and in slightly different manners, for each one of forty motorcar drivers facing two opposite directions, while at the

same time diminishing for forty more who have got their backs to it, meanwhile remembering to loom over each single one at the right moment: and to do this minute after minute, hour after hour, from daybreak till nightfall or long after?

For my road had become a busy one; it worked all day long under almost continual traffic. It worked, and I worked. I did not jounce and bounce so much any more, but I had to run faster and faster: to grow enormously, to loom in a split second, to shrink to nothing, all in a hurry, without time to enjoy the action, and without rest: over and over and over.

Very few of the drivers bothered to look at me, not even a seeing glance. They seemed, indeed, not to see any more. They merely stared ahead. They seemed to believe that they were 'going somewhere'. Little mirrors were affixed to the front of their cars, at which they glanced to see where they had been; then they stared ahead again. I had thought that only beetles had this delusion of Progress. Beetles are always rushing about, and never looking up. I had always had a pretty low opinion of beetles. But at least they let me be.

I confess that sometimes, in the blessed nights of darkness with no moon to silver my crown and no stars occluding with my branches, when I could rest, I would think seriously of escaping my obligation to the general Order of Things: of *failing to move*. No, not seriously. Half-seriously. It was mere weariness. If even a silly, three-year-old, female pussy willow at the foot of the hill accepted her responsibility, and jounced and rolled and accelerated and grew and shrank for each motor-car on the road, was I, an oak, to shirk? Noblesse oblige, and I trust I have never dropped an acorn that did not know its duty.

For fifty or sixty years, when, I have upheld the Order of Things, and have done my share in supporting the human creatures' illusion that they are 'going somewhere'. And I am not unwilling to do so. But a truly terrible thing has occurred, which I wish to protest.

I do not mind going two directions at once; I do not mind growing and shrinking simultaneously; I do not mind moving,

even at the disagreeable rate of sixty or seventy miles an hour. I am ready to go on doing all these things until I am felled or bulldozed. They're my job. But I do object, passionately, to being made eternal.

Eternity is none of my business. I am an oak, no more, no less. I have my duty, and I do it; I have my pleasures, and enjoy them, though they are fewer, since the birds are fewer, and the wind's foul. But long-lived though I may be, impermanence is my right. Mortality is my privilege. And it has been taken from me.

It was taken from me on a rainy evening in March last year.

Fits and bursts of cars, as usual, filled the rapidly moving road in both directions. I was so busy hurtling along, enlarging, looming, diminishing, and the light was failing so fast, that I scarcely noticed what was happening until it happened. One of the drivers of one of the cars evidently felt that his need to 'go somewhere' was exceptionally urgent, and so attempted to place his car in front of the car in front of it. This maneuver involves a temporary slanting of the Direction of the Road and a displacement onto the far side, the side which normally runs the other direction (and may I say that I admire the road very highly for its skill in executing such maneuvers, which must be difficult for an unliving creature, a mere making). Another car, however, happened to be quite near the urgent one, and facing it, as it changed sides; and the road could not do anything about it, being already overcrowded. To avoid impact with the facing car, the urgent car totally violated the Direction of the Road, swinging it around to North-South in its own terms, and so forcing me to leap directly at it. I had no choice. I had to move, and move fast – eighty-five miles an hour. I leapt: I loomed enormous, larger than I have ever loomed before. And then I hit the car.

I lost a considerable piece of bark, and, what's more serious, a fair bit of cambium layer; but as I was seventy-two feet tall and about nine feet in girth at the point of impact, no real harm was done. My branches trembled with the shock enough that a

last-year's robin's nest was dislodged and fell; and I was so shaken that I groaned. It is the only time in my life that I have ever said anything out loud.

The motorcar screamed horribly. It was smashed by my blow, squashed, in fact. Its hinder parts were not much affected, but the forequarters knotted up and knurled together like an old root, and little bright bits of it flew all about and lay like brittle rain.

The driver had no time to say anything; I killed him instantly.

It is not this that I protest. I had to kill him. I had no choice, and therefore have no regret. What I protest, what I cannot endure, is this: as I leapt at him, he saw me. He looked up at last. He saw me as I have never been seen before, not even by a child, not even in the days when people looked at things. He saw me whole, and saw nothing else – then, or ever.

He saw me under the aspect of eternity. He confused me with eternity. And because he died in that moment of false vision, because it can never change, I am caught in it, eternally.

This is unendurable. I cannot uphold such an illusion. If the human creatures will not understand Relativity, very well; but they must understand Relatedness.

If it is necessary to the Order of Things, I will kill drivers of cars, though killing is not a duty usually required of oaks. But it is unjust to require me to play the part, not of the killer only, but of death. For I am not death. I am life: I am mortal.

If they wish to see death visibly in the world, that is their business, not mine. I will not act Eternity for them. Let them not turn to the trees for death. If that is what they want to see, let them look into one another's eyes and see it there.

THE ONES WHO WALK AWAY
FROM OMELAS

(Variations on a theme by William James)

The central idea of this psychomyth, the scapegoat, turns up in Dostoyevsky's Brothers Karamazov, *and several people have asked me, rather suspiciously, why I gave the credit to William James. The fact is, I haven't been able to re-read Dostoyevsky much as I loved him, since I was twenty-five, and I'd simply forgotten he used the idea. But when I met it in James's 'The Moral Philosopher and the Moral Life', it was with a shock of recognition. Here is how James puts it:*

Or if the hypothesis were offered us of a world in which Messrs Fourier's and Bellamy's and Morris's utopias should all be outdone, and millions kept permanently happy on the one simple condition that a certain lost soul on the far-off edge of things should lead a life of lonely torment, what except a specifical and independent sort of emotion can it be which would make us immediately feel, even though an impulse arose within us to clutch at the happiness so offered, how hideous a thing would be its enjoyment when deliberately accepted as the fruit of such a bargain?

The dilemma of the American conscience can hardly be better stated. Dostoyevsky was a great artist, and a radical one, but his early social radicalism reversed itself, leaving him a violent reactionary. Whereas the American James, who seems so mild, so naïvely gentlemanly — look how he says 'us', assuming all his readers are as decent as himself! — was, and remained, and remains, a genuinely radical thinker. Directly after the 'lost soul' passage he goes on,

All the higher, more penetrating ideals are revolutionary. They present themselves far less in the guise of effects of past experience than in that of probable causes of future experience, factors to which the environment and the lessons it has so far taught us must learn to bend.

The application of those two sentences to this story, and to science fiction, and to all thinking about the future, is quite direct. Ideals as 'the probable causes of the future experience' — that is a subtle and an exhilarating remark!

Of course I didn't read James and sit down and say, Now I'll write a story about that 'lost soul'. It seldom works that simply. I sat down and started a story, just because I felt like it, with nothing but the word 'Omelas' in mind. It came from a road sign: Salem (Oregon) backwards. Don't you read road signs backwards? POTS. WOLS nerdlihc. Ocsicnarf Nas . . . Salem equals schelomo equals salaam equals Peace. Melas. O melas, Omelas. Homme hélas. 'Where do you get your ideas from, Ms Le Guin?' From forgetting Dostoyevsky and reading road signs backwards naturally. Where else?

With a clamor of bells that set the swallows soaring, the Festival of Summer came to the city Omelas, bright-towered by the sea. The rigging of the boats in harbor sparkled with flags. In the streets between houses with red roofs and painted walls, between old moss-grown gardens and under avenues of trees, past great parks and public buildings, processions moved. Some were decorous: old people in long stiff robes of mauve and grey, grave master workmen, quiet, merry women carrying their babies and chatting as they walked. In other streets the music beat faster, a shimmering of gong and tambourine, and the people went dancing, the procession was a dance. Children dodged in and out, their high calls rising like the swallows' crossing flights over the music and the singing. All the processions wound towards the north side of the city, where on the

great water-meadow called the Green Fields boys and girls, naked in the bright air, with mud-stained feet and ankles and long, lithe arms, exercised their restive horses before the race. The horses wore no gear at all but a halter without bit. Their manes were braided with streamers of silver, gold, and green. They flared their nostrils and pranced and boasted to one another; they were vastly excited, the horse being the only animal who has adopted our ceremonies as his own. Far off to the north and west the mountains stood up half encircling Omelas on her bay. The air of morning was so clear that the snow still crowning the Eighteen Peaks burned with white-gold fire across the miles of sunlit air, under the dark blue of the sky. There was just enough wind to make the banners that marked the racecourse snap and flutter now and then. In the silence of the broad green meadows one could hear the music winding through the city streets, farther and nearer and ever approaching, a cheerful faint sweetness of the air that from time to time trembled and gathered together and broke out into the great joyous clanging of the bells.

Joyous! How is one to tell about joy? How describe the citizens of Omelas?

They were not simple folk, you see, though they were happy. But we do not say the words of cheer much any more. All smiles have become archaic. Given a description such as this one tends to make certain assumptions. Given a description such as this one tends to look next for the King, mounted on a splendid stallion and surrounded by his noble knights, or perhaps in a golden litter borne by great-muscled slaves. But there was no king. They did not use swords, or keep slaves. They were not barbarians. I do not know the rules and laws of their society, but I suspect that they were singularly few. As they did without monarchy and slavery, so they also got on without the stock exchange, the advertisement, the secret police, and the bomb. Yet I repeat that these were not simple folk, not dulcet shepherds, noble savages, bland utopians. They were not less complex than us. The trouble is that we have a bad habit,

encouraged by pedants and sophisticates, of considering happiness as something rather stupid. Only pain is intellectual, only evil interesting. This is the treason of the artist: a refusal to admit the banality of evil and the terrible boredom of pain. If you can't lick 'em, join 'em. If it hurts, repeat it. But to praise despair is to condemn delight, to embrace violence is to lose hold of everything else. We have almost lost hold; we can no longer describe a happy man, nor make any celebration of joy. How can I tell you about the people of Omelas? They were not naïve and happy children – though their children were, in fact, happy. They were mature, intelligent, passionate adults whose lives were not wretched. O miracle! but I wish I could describe it better. I wish I could convince you. Omelas sounds in my words like a city in a fairy tale, long ago and far away, once upon a time. Perhaps it would be best if you imagined it as your own fancy bids, assuming it will rise to the occasion, for certainly I cannot suit you all. For instance, how about technology? I think that there would be no cars or helicopters in and above the streets; this follows from the fact that the people of Omelas are happy people. Happiness is based on a just discrimination of what is necessary, what is neither necessary nor destructive, and what is destructive. In the middle category, however – that of the unnecessary but undestructive, that of comfort, luxury, exuberance, etc, etc. – they could perfectly well have central heating, subway trains, washing machines, and all kinds of marvellous devices not yet invented here, floating light-sources, fuelless power, a cure for the common cold. Or they could have none of that: it doesn't matter. As you like it. I incline to think that people from towns up and down the coast have been coming in to Omelas during the last days before the Festival on very fast little trains and double-decked trams, and that the train station of Omelas is actually the handsomest building in town, though plainer than the magnificent Farmers' Market. But even granted trains, I fear that Omelas so far strikes some of you as goody-goody. Smiles, bells, parades, horses, bleh. If so, please add an orgy. If

an orgy would help, don't hesitate. Let us not, however, have temples from which issue beautiful nude priests and priestesses already half in ecstasy and ready to copulate with any man or woman, lover or stranger, who desires union with the deep god-head of the blood, although that was my first idea. But really it would be better not to have any temples in Omelas – at least, not manned temples. Religion yes, clergy no. Surely the beauti-ful nudes can just wander about offering themselves like divine soufflés to the hunger of the needy and the rapture of the flesh Let them join the processions. Let tambourines be struck above the copulations, and the glory of desire be proclaimed upon the gongs, and (a not unimportant point) let the offspring of these delightful rituals be beloved and looked after by all. One thing I know there is none of in Omelas is guilt. But what else should there be? I thought at first there were no drugs, but that is puritanical. For those who like it, the faint insistent sweet-ness of *drooz* may perfume the ways of the City, *drooz* which first brings a great lightness and brilliance to the mind and limbs, and then after some hours a dreamy languor, and won-derful visions at last of the very arcana and inmost secrets of the Universe, as well as exciting the pleasure of sex beyond all belief; and it is not habit-forming. For more modest tastes I think there ought to be beer. What else, what else belongs in the joyous city? The sense of victory, surely, the celebration of courage. But as we did without clergy, let us do without soldiers. The joy built upon successful slaughter is not the right kind of joy; it will not do, it is fearful and it is trivial. A boundless and generous contentment, a magnanimous triumph felt not against some outer enemy but in communion with the finest and fairest in the souls of all men everywhere and the splendor of the world's summer: this is what swells the hearts of the people of Omelas, and the victory they celebrate is that of life. I really don't think many of them need to take *drooz*.

Most of the processsions have reached the Green Fields by now. A marvelous smell of cooking goes forth from the red and blue tents of the provisioners. The faces of small children are

amiably sticky; in the benign grey beard of a man a couple of crumbs of rich pastry are entangled. The youths and girls have mounted their horses and are beginning to group around the starting line of the course. An old woman, small, fat, and laughing, is passing out flowers from a basket, and tall young men wear her flowers in their shining hair. A child of nine or ten sits at the edge of the crowd, alone, playing on a wooden flute. People pause to listen, and they smile, but they do not speak to him for he never ceases playing and never sees them, his dark eyes wholly rapt in the sweet, thin magic of the tune.

He finishes, and slowly lowers his hands holding the wooden flute.

As if that little private silence were the signal, all at once a trumpet sounds from the pavilion near the starting line: imperious, melancholy, piercing. The horses rear on their slender legs, and some of them neigh in answer. Sober-faced, the young riders stroke the horses' necks and soothe them, whispering, 'Quiet, quiet, there my beauty, my hope . . .' They begin to form in rank along the starting line. The crowds along the racecourse are like a field of grass and flowers in the wind. The Festival of Summer has begun.

Do you believe? Do you accept the festival, the city, the joy? No? Then let me describe one more thing.

In a basement under one of the beautiful public buildings of Omelas, or perhaps in the cellar of one of its spacious private homes, there is a room. It has one locked door, and no window. A little light seeps in dustily between cracks in the boards, secondhand from a cobwebbed window somewhere across the cellar. In one corner of the little room a couple of mops, with stiff, clotted, foul-smelling heads, stand near a rusty bucket. The floor is dirt, a little damp to the touch, as cellar dirt usually is. The room is about three paces long and two wide: a mere broom closet or disused tool room. In the room a child is sitting. It could be a boy or a girl. It looks about six, but actually is nearly ten. It is feeble-minded. Perhaps it was born defective, or perhaps it has become imbecile through fear, mal-

nutrition, and neglect. It picks its nose and occasionally fumbles vaguely with its toes or genitals, as it sits hunched in the corner farthest from the bucket and the two mops. It is afraid of the mops. It finds them horrible. It shuts its eyes, but it know the mops are still standing there; and the door is locked; and nobody will come. The door is always locked; and nobody ever comes, except that sometimes – the child has no under-standing of time or interval – sometimes the door rattles terribly and opens, and a person, or several people, are there. One of them may come in and kick the child to make it stand up. The others never come close, but peer in at it with frightened, disgusted eyes. The food bowl and the water jug are hastily filled, the door is locked, the eyes disappear. The people at the door never say anything, but the child, who has not always lived in the tool room, and can remember sunlight and its mother's voice, sometimes speaks. 'I will be good,' it says. 'Please let me out. I will be good!' They never answer. The child used to scream for help at night, and cry a good deal, but now it only makes a kind of whining, 'eh-haa, eh-haa', and it speaks less and less often. It is so thin there are no calves to its legs; its belly protrudes; it lives on a half-bowl of corn meal and grease a day. It is naked. Its buttocks and thighs are a mass of festered sores, as it sits in its own excrement continually.

They all know it is there, all the people of Omelas. Some of them have come to see it, others are content merely to know it is there. They all know that it has to be there. Some of them understand why, and some do not, but they all understand that their happiness, the beauty of their city, the tenderness of their friendships, the health of their children, the wisdom of their scholars, the skill of their makers, even the abundance of their harvest and the kindly weathers of their skies, depend wholly on this child's abominable misery.

This is usually explained to children when they are between eight and twelve, whenever they seem capable of under-standing; and most of those who come to see the child are young people, though often enough an adult comes, or comes

back, to see the child. No matter how well the matter has been explained to them, these young spectators are always shocked and sickened at the sight. They feel disgust, which they had thought themselves superior to. They feel anger, outrage, impotence, despite all the explanations. They would like to do something for the child. But there is nothing they can do. If the child were brought up into the sunlight out of that vile place, if it were cleaned and fed and comforted, that would be a good thing, indeed; but if it were done, in that day and hour all the prosperity and beauty and delight of Omelas would wither and be destroyed. Those are the terms. To exchange all the goodness and grace of every life in Omelas for that single, small improvement: to throw away the happiness of thousands for the chance of the happiness of one: that would be to let guilt within the walls indeed.

The terms are strict and absolute; there may not even be a kind word spoken to the child.

Often the young people go home in tears, or in a tearless rage, when they have seen the child and faced this terrible paradox. They may brood over it for weeks or years. But as time goes on they begin to realize that even if the child could be released, it would not get much good of its freedom: a little vague pleasure of warmth and food, no doubt, but little more. It is too degraded and imbecile to know any real joy. It has been afraid too long ever to be free of fear. Its habits are too uncouth for it to respond to humane treatment. Indeed, after so long it would probably be wretched without walls about it to protect it, and darkness for its eyes, and its own excrement to sit in. Their tears at the bitter injustice dry when they begin to perceive the terrible justice of reality, and to accept it. Yet it is their tears and anger, the trying of their generosity and the acceptance of their helplessness, which are perhaps the true source of the splendor of their lives. Theirs is no vapid, irresponsible happiness. They know that they, like the child, are not free. They know compassion. It is the existence of the child, and their knowledge of its existence, that makes possible the nobility of

their architecture, the poignancy of their music, the profundity of their science. It is because of the child that they are so gentle with children. They know that if the wretched one were not there snivelling in the dark, the other one, the flute-player, could make no joyful music as the young riders line up in their beauty for the race in the sunlight of the first morning of summer.

Now do you believe in them? Are they not more credible? But there is one more thing to tell, and this is quite incredible.

At times one of the adolescent girls or boys who go to see the child does not go home to weep or rage, does not, in fact, go home at all. Sometimes also a man or woman much older falls silent for a day or two, and then leaves home. These people go out into the street, and walk straight out of the city of Omelas, through the beautiful gates. They keep walking across the farmlands of Omelas. Each one goes alone, youth or girl, man or woman. Night falls; the traveler must pass down village streets, between the houses with yellow-lit windows, and on out into the darkness of the fields. Each alone, they go west or north, towards the mountains. They go on. They leave Omelas, they walk ahead into the darkness, and they do not come back. The place they go towards is a place even less imaginable to most of us than the city of happiness. I cannot describe it at all. It is possible that it does not exist. But they seem to know where they are going, the ones who walk away from Omelas.

THE DAY BEFORE THE REVOLUTION

In memoriam Paul Goodman, 1911–1972

My novel The Dispossessed *is about a small worldful of people who call themselves Odonians. The name is taken from the founder of their society, Odo, who lived several generations before the time of the novel, and who therefore doesn't get into the action – except implicitly, in that all the action started with her.*

Odonianism is anarchism. Not the bomb-in-the-pocket stuff, which is terrorism, whatever name it tries to dignify itself with; not the social-Darwinist economic 'libertarianism' of the far right; but anarchism, as prefigured in early Taoist thought, and expounded by Shelley and Kropotkin, Goldman and Goodman. Anarchism's principal target is the authoritarian State (capitalist or socialist); its principal moral-practical theme is cooperation (solidarity, mutual aid). It is the most idealistic, and to me the most interesting, of all political theories.

To embody it in a novel, which had not been done before, was a long and hard job for me, and absorbed me totally for many months. When it was done I felt lost, exiled – a displaced person. I was very grateful, therefore, when Odo came out of the shadows and across the gulf of Probability, and wanted a story written, not about the world she made, but about herself.

This story is about one of the ones who walked away from Omelas.

The speaker's voice was as loud as empty beer-trucks in a stone street, and the people at the meeting were jammed up close, cobblestones, that great voice booming over them. Taviri was

somewhere on the other side of the hall. She had to get to him.
She wormed and pushed her way among the dark-clothed,
close-packed people. She did not hear the words, nor see the
faces: only the booming, and the bodies pressed one behind the
other. She could not see Taviri, she was too short. A broad
black-vested belly and chest loomed up, blocking her way. She
must get through to Taviri. Sweating, she jabbed fiercely with
her fist. It was like hitting stone, he did not move at all, but the
huge lungs let out right over her head a prodigious noise, a
bellow. She cowered. Then she understood that the bellow had
not been at her. Others were shouting. The speaker had said
something, something fine about taxes or shadows. Thrilled,
she joined the shouting – 'Yes! Yes!' – and shoving on, came
out easily into the open expanse of the Regimental Drill Field
in Parheo. Overhead the evening sky lay deep and colorless,
and all around her nodded the tall weeds with dry, white, close-
floreted heads. She had never known what they were called.
The flowers nodded above her head, swaying in the wind that
always blew across the fields in the dusk. She ran among them,
and they whipped lithe aside and stood up again swaying,
silent. Taviri stood among the tall weeds in his good suit, the
dark grey one that made him look like a professor or a play-
actor, harshly elegant. He did not look happy, but he was
laughing, and saying something to her. The sound of his voice
made her cry, and she reached out to catch hold of his hand, but
she did not stop, quite. She could not stop. 'Oh, Taviri,' she
said, 'it's just on there!' The queer sweet smell of the white
weeds was heavy as she went on. There were thorns, tangles
underfoot, there were slopes, pits. She feared to fall, to fall, she
stopped.

Sun, bright morning-glare, straight in the eyes, relentless. She
had forgotten to pull the blind last night. She turned her back
on the sun, but the right side wasn't comfortable. No use. Day.
She sighed twice, sat up, got her legs over the edge of the bed,
and sat hunched in her nightdress looking down at her feet.

The toes, compressed by a lifetime of cheap shoes, were

almost square where they touched each other, and bulged out above in corns; the nails were discolored and shapeless. Between the knob-like anklebones ran fine, dry wrinkles. The brief little plain at the base of the toes had kept its delicacy, but the skin was the color of mud, and knotted veins crossed the instep. Disgusting. Sad, depressing. Mean. Pitiful. She tried on all the words, and they all fit, like hideous little hats. Hideous: yes, that one too. To look at oneself and find it hideous, what a job! But then, when she hadn't been hideous, had she sat around and stared at herself like this? Not much! A proper body's not an object, not an implement, not a belonging to be admired, it's just you, yourself. Only when it's no longer you, but yours, a thing owned, do you worry about it – Is it in good shape? Will it do? Will it last?

'Who cares?' said Laia fiercely, and stood up.

It made her giddy to stand up suddenly. She had to put out her hand to the bed-table, for she dreaded falling. At that she thought of reaching out to Taviri, in the dream.

What had he said? She could not remember. She was not sure if she had even touched his hand. She frowned, trying to force memory. It had been so long since she had dreamed about Taviri; and now not even to remember what he had said!

It was gone, it was gone. She stood there hunched in her nightdress, frowning, one hand on the bed-table. How long was it since she had thought of him – let alone dreamed of him – even thought of him, as 'Taviri'? How long since she had said his name?

Asieo said. When Asieo and I were in prison in the North. Before I met Asieo. Asieo's theory of reciprocity. Oh yes, she talked about him, talked about him too much no doubt, maundered, dragged him in. But as 'Asieo', the last name, the public man. The private man was gone, utterly gone. There were so few left who had even known him. They had all used to be in jail. One laughed about it in those days, all the friends in all the jails. But they weren't even there, these days. They were in the prison cemeteries. Or in the common graves.

'Oh, oh my dear,' Laia said out loud, and she sank down onto the bed again because she could not stand up under the remembrance of those first weeks in the Fort, in the cell, those first weeks of the nine years in the Fort in Drio, in the cell, those first weeks after they told her that Asieo had been killed in the fighting in Capitol Square and had been buried with the Fourteen Hundred in the lime-ditches behind Oring Gate. In the cell. Her hands fell into the old position on her lap, the left clenched and locked inside the grip of the right, the right thumb working back and forth a little pressing and rubbing on the knuckle of the left first finger. Hours, days, nights. She had thought of them all, each one, each one of the Fourteen Hundred, how they lay, how the quicklime worked on the flesh, how the bones touched in the burning dark. Who touched him? How did the slender bones of the hand lie now? Hours, years.

'Taviri, I have never forgotten you!' she whispered, and the stupidity of it brought her back to morning light and the rumpled bed. Of course she hadn't forgotten him. These things go without saying betwen husband and wife. There were her ugly old feet flat on the floor again, just as before. She had got nowhere at all, she had gone in a circle. She stood up with a grunt of effort and disapproval, and went to the closet for her dressing gown.

The young people went about the halls of the House in becoming immodesty, but she was too old for that. She didn't want to spoil some young man's breakfast with the sight of her. Besides, they had grown up in the principle of freedom of dress and sex and all the rest, and she hadn't. All she had done was invent it. It's not the same.

Like speaking of Asieo as 'my husband'. They winced. The word she should use as a good Odonian, of course, was 'partner'. But why the hell did she have to be a good Odonian?

She shuffled down the hall to the bathrooms. Mairo was there, washing her hair in a lavatory. Laia looked at the long, sleek, wet hank with admiration. She got out of the House so seldom now that she didn't know when she had last seen a

respectably shaven scalp, but still the sight of a full head of hair
gave her pleasure, vigorous pleasure. How many times had she
been jeered at *Longhair, longhair*, had her hair pulled by
policemen or young toughs, had her hair shaved off down to the
scalp by a grinning soldier at each new prison? And then had
grown it all over again, through the fuzz, to the frizz, to the
curls, to the mane . . . In the old days. For God's love, couldn't
she think of anything today but the old days?

Dressed, her bed made, she went down to commons. It was a
good breakfast, but she had never got her appetite back since
the damned stroke. She drank two cups of herb tea, but couldn't
finish the piece of fruit she had taken. How she had craved fruit
as a child badly enough to steal it; and in the Fort – oh, for
God's love stop it! She smiled and replied to the greetings and
friendly inquiries of the other breakfasters and big Aevi who
was serving the counter this morning. It was he who had
tempted her with the peach, 'Look at this, I've been saving it
for you,' and how could she refuse? Anyway she had always
loved fruit, and never got enough; once when she was six or
seven she had stolen a piece off a vendor's cart in River Street.
But it was hard to eat when everyone was talking so excitedly.
There was news from Thu, real news. She was inclined to
discount it at first, being wary of enthusiasms, but after she had
read the article in the paper, and read between the lines of it,
she thought, with a strange kind of certainty, deep but cold,
Why, this is it; it has come. And in Thu, not here. Thu will
break before this country does; the Revolution will first prevail
there. As if that mattered! There will be no more nations. And
yet it did matter somehow, it made her a little cold and sad –
envious, in fact. Of all the infinite stupidities. She did not join
in the talk much, and soon got up to go back to her room,
feeling sorry for herself. She could not share their excitement.
She was out of it, really out of it. It's not easy, she said to
herself in justification, laboriously climbing the stairs, to accept
being out of it when you've been in it, in the center of it, for
fifty years. Oh, for God's love. Whining!

She got the stairs and the self-pity behind her, entering her room. It was a good room, and it was good to be by herself. It was a great relief. Even if it wasn't strictly fair. Some of the kids in the attics were living five to a room no bigger than this. There were always more people wanting to live in an Odonian House than could be properly accommodated. She had this big room all to herself only because she was an old woman who had had a stroke. And maybe because she was Odo. If she hadn't been Odo, but merely the old woman with a stroke, would she have had it? Very likely. After all, who the hell wanted to room with a drooling old woman? But it was hard to be sure. Favoritism, elitism, leader-worship, they crept back and cropped out everywhere. But she had never hoped to see them eradicated in her lifetime, in one generation; only Time works the great changes. Meanwhile this was a nice, large, sunny room, proper for a drooling old woman who had started a world revolution.

Her secretary would be coming in an hour to help her despatch the day's work. She shuffled over to the desk, a beautiful, big piece, a present from the Nio Cabinetmakers' Syndicate because somebody had heard her remark once that the only piece of furniture she had ever really longed for was a desk with drawers and enough room on top . . . damn, the top was practically covered with papers with notes clipped to them, mostly in Noi's small clear handwriting: Urgent. – Northern Provinces. – Consult w/R.T.?

Her own handwriting had never been the same since Asieo's death. It was odd, when you thought about it. After all, within five years after his death she had writen the whole *Analogy*. And there were those letters, which the tall guard with the watery grey eyes, what was his name, never mind, had smuggled out of the Fort for her for two years. *The Prison Letters* they called them now, there were a dozen different editions of them. All that stuff, the letters which people kept telling her were so full of 'spiritual strength' – which probably meant she had been lying herself blue in the face when she wrote them, trying to keep her spirits up – and the *Analogy* which was certainly

the solidest intellectual work she had ever done, all of that had been written in the Fort in Drio, in the cell, after Asieo's death. One had to do something, and in the Fort they let one have paper and pens ... But it had all been written in the hasty, scribbling hand which she had never felt was hers, not her own like the round, black scrollings of the manuscript of *Society Without Government,* forty-five years old. Taviri had taken not only her body's and her heart's desire to the quicklime with him, but even her good clear handwriting.

But he had left her the Revolution.

How brave of you to go on, to work, to write, in prison, after such a defeat for the Movement, after your partner's death, people had used to say. Damn fools. What else had there been to do? Bravery, courage — what was courage? She had never figured it out. Not fearing, some said. Fearing yet going on, others said. But what could one do but go on? Had one any real choice, ever?

To die was merely to go on in another direction.

If you wanted to come home you had to keep going on, that was what she meant when she wrote 'True journey is return', but it had never been more than an intuition, and she was farther than ever now from being able to rationalize it. She bent down, too suddenly, so that she grunted a little at the creak in her bones, and began to root in a bottom drawer of the desk. Her hand came on an age-softened folder and drew it out, recognizing it by touch before sight confirmed: the manuscript of *Syndical Organization in Revolutionary Transition.* He had printed the title on the folder and written his name under it, Taviri Odo Asieo, IX 741. There was an elegant handwriting, every letter well-formed, bold, and fluent. But he had preferred to use a voiceprinter. The manuscript was all in voiceprint, and high quality too, hesitancies adjusted and idiosyncrasies of speech normalized. You couldn't see there how he had said 'o' deep in his throat as they did on the North Coast. There was nothing of him there but his mind. She had nothing of him at all except his name written on the folder. She hadn't kept his

letters, it was sentimental to keep letters. Besides, she never
kept anything. She couldn't think of anything that she had ever
owned for more than a few years, except this ramshackle old
body, of course, and she was stuck with that . . .

Dualizing again. 'She' and 'it'. Age and illness made one
dualist, made one escapist; the mind insisted, *It's not me, it's
not me.* But it was. Maybe the mystics could detach mind from
body, she had always rather wistfully envied them the chance,
without hope of emulating them. Escape had never been her
game. She had sought for freedom here, now, body and soul.

First self-pity, then self-praise, and here she still sat, for
God's love, holding Asieo's name in her hand, why? Didn't she
know his name without looking it up? What was wrong with
her? She raised the folder to her lips and kissed the handwritten
name firmly and squarely, replaced the folder in the back of the
bottom drawer, shut the drawer, and straightened up in the
chair. Her right hand tingled. She scratched it, and then shook
it in the air, spitefully. It had never quite got over the stroke.
Neither had her right leg, or right eye, or the right corner of
her mouth. They were sluggish, inept, they tingled. They
made her feel like a robot with a short circuit.

And time was getting on, Noi would be coming, what had she
been doing ever since breakfast?

She got up so hastily that she lurched, and grabbed at the
chairback to make sure she did not fall. She went down the hall
to the bathroom and looked in the big mirror there. Her grey
knot was loose and droopy, she hadn't done it up well before
breakfast. She struggled with it a while. It was hard to keep
her arms up in the air. Amai, running in to piss, stopped and
said, 'Let me do it!' and knotted it up tight and neat in no time,
with her round, strong, pretty fingers, smiling and silent. Amai
was twenty, less than a third of Laia's age. Her parents had
both been members of the Movement, one killed in the insur-
rection of '60, the other still recruiting in the South Provinces.
Amai had grown up in Odonian Houses, born to the Revolu-
tion, a true daughter of anarchy. And so quiet and free and

beautiful a child, enough to make you cry when you thought: this is what we worked for, this is what we meant, this is it, here she is, alive, the kindly, lovely future.

Laia Asieo Odo's right eye wept several little tears, as she stood between the lavatories and the latrines having her hair done up by the daughter she had not borne; but her left eye, the strong one, did not weep, nor did it know what the right eye did.

She thanked Amai and hurried back to her room. She had noticed, in the mirror, a stain on her collar. Peach juice, probably. Damned old dribbler. She didn't want Noi to come in and find her with drool on her collar.

As the clean shirt went on over her head, she thought, What's so special about Noi?

She fastened the collar-frogs with her left hand, slowly.

Noi was thirty or so, a slight, muscular fellow with a soft voice and alert dark eyes. That's what was special about Noi. It was that simple. Good old sex. She had never been drawn to a fair man or a fat one, or the tall fellows with big biceps, never, not even when she was fourteen and fell in love with every passing fart. Dark, spare, and fiery, that was the recipe. Taviri, of course. This boy wasn't a patch on Taviri for brains, nor even for looks, but there it was: she didn't want him to see her with dribble on her collar and her hair coming undone.

Her thin, grey hair.

Noi came in, just pausing in the open doorway – my God, she hadn't even shut the door while changing her shirt! She looked at him and saw herself. The old woman.

You could brush your hair and change your shirt, or you could wear last week's shirt and last night's braids, or you could put on cloth of gold and dust your shaven scalp with diamond powder. None of it would make the slightest difference. The old woman would look a little less, or a little more, grotesque.

One keeps oneself neat out of mere decency, mere sanity, awareness of other people.

And finally even that goes, and one dribbles unashamed.

'Good morning,' the young man said in his gentle voice.
'Hello, Noi.'

No, by God, it was *not* out of mere decency. Decency be
damned. Because the man she had loved, and to whom her age
would not have mattered – because he was dead, must she pre-
tend she had no sex? Must she suppress the truth, like a
damned puritan authoritarian? Even six months ago, before the
stroke, she had made men look at her and like to look at her;
and now, though she could give no pleasure, by God she could
please herself.

When she was six years old, and Papa's friend Gadeo used to
come by to talk politics with Papa after dinner, she would put
on the gold-colored necklace that Mama had found on a trash
heap and brought home for her. It was so short that it always
got hidden under her collar where nobody could see it. She
liked it that way. She knew she had it on. She sat on the door-
step and listened to them talk, and knew that she looked nice
for Gadeo. He was dark, with white teeth that flashed. Some-
times he called her 'pretty Laia'. 'There's my pretty Laia!'
Sixty-six years ago.

'What? My head's dull. I had a terrible night.' It was true.
She had slept even less than usual.

'I was asking if you'd seen the papers this morning.'

She nodded.

'Pleased about Soinehe?'

Soinehe was the province in Thu which had declared its
secession from the Thuvian State last night.

He was pleased about it. His white teeth flashed in his dark,
alert face. Pretty Laia.

'Yes. And apprehensive.'

'I know. But it's the real thing, this time. It's the beginning
of the end of the Government in Thu. They haven't even tried
to order troops into Soinehe, you know. It would merely pro-
voke the soldiers into rebellion sooner, and they know it.'

She agreed with him. She herself had felt that certainty. But

she could not share his delight. After a lifetime of living on hope because there is nothing but hope, one loses the taste for victory. A real sense of triumph must be preceded by real despair. She had unlearned despair a long time ago. There were no more triumphs. One went on.

'Shall we do those letters today?'

'All right. Which letters?'

'To the people in the North,' he said without impatience.

'In the North?'

'Parheo, Oaidun.'

She had been born in Parheo, the dirty city on the dirty river. She had not come here to the capital till she was twenty-two and ready to bring the Revolution. Though in those days, before she and the others had thought it through, it had been a very green and puerile revolution. Strikes for better wages, representation for women. Votes and wages – Power and Money, for the love of God! Well, one does learn a little, after all, in fifty years.

But then one must forget it all.

'Start with Oaidun,' she said, sitting down in the armchair. Noi was at the desk ready to work. He read out excerpts from the letters she was to answer. She tried to pay attention, and succeeded well enough that she dictated one whole letter and started on another. 'Remember that at this stage your brotherhood is vulnerable to the threat of . . . no, to the danger . . . to . . .' She groped till Noi suggested, 'The danger of leader-worship?'

'All right. And that nothing is so soon corrupted by power-seeking as altruism. No. And that nothing corrupts altruism – no. O for God's love you know what I'm trying to say, Noi, you write it. They know it too, it's just the same old stuff, why can't they read my boooks!'

'Touch,' Noi said gently, smiling, citing one of the central Odonian themes.

'All right, but I'm tired of being touched. If you'll write the

letter I'll sign it, but I can't be bothered with it this morning.'
He was looking at her with a little question or concern. She
said, irritable, 'There is something else I have to do!'

When Noi had gone she sat down at the desk and moved the
papers about, pretending to be doing something, because she
had been startled, frightened, by the words she had said. She
had nothing else to do. She never had had anything else to do.
This was her work: her lifework. The speaking tours and the
meetings and the streets were out of reach for her now, but she
could still write, and that was her work. And anyhow if she had
had anything else to do, Noi would have known it; he kept her
schedule, and tactfully reminded her of things, like the visit
from the foreign students this afternoon.

Oh, damn. She liked the young, and there was always some-
thing to learn from a foreigner, but she was tired of new faces,
and tired of being on view. She learned from them, but they
didn't learn from her; they had learnt all she had to teach long
ago, from her books, from the Movement. They just came to
look, as if she were the Great Tower in Rodarred, or the
Canyon of the Tulaevea. A phenomenon, a monument. They
were awed, adoring. She snarled at them: Think your own
thoughts! – That's not anarchism, that's mere obscurantism. –
You don't think liberty and discipline are incompatible, do
you? – They accepted their tongue-lashing meekly as children,
gratefully, as if she were some kind of All-Mother, the idol of
the Big Sheltering Womb. She! She who had mined the ship-
yards at Seissero, and had cursed Premier Inoilte to his face in
front of a crowd of seven thousand, telling him he would have
cut off his own balls and had them bronzed and sold as souve-
nirs, if he thought there was any profit in it – she who had
screeched, and sworn, and kicked policemen, and spat at
priests, and pissed in public on the big brass plaque in Capitol
Square that said HERE WAS FOUNDED THE SOVEREIGN NATION
STATE OF A–IO ETC ETC, psssssssss to all that! And now she

was everybody's grandmama, the dear old lady, the sweet old monument, come worship at the womb. The fire's out, boys, it's safe to come up close.

'No, I won't,' Laia said out loud. 'I will not.' She was not self-conscious about talking to herself, because she always had talked to herself. 'Laia's invisible audience,' Taviri had used to say, as she went through the room muttering. 'You needn't come, I won't be here,' she told the invisible audience now. She had just decided what it was she had to do. She had to go out. To go into the streets.

It was inconsiderate to disappoint the foreign students. It was erratic, typically senile. It was unOdonian. Psssssss to all that. What was the good working for freedom all your life and ending up without any freedom at all? She would go out for a walk.

'What is an anarchist? One who, choosing, accepts the responsibility of choice.'

On the way downstairs she decided, scowling, to stay and see the foreign students. But then she would go out.

They were very young students, very earnest: doe-eyed, shaggy, charming creatures from the Western Hemisphere, Benbili and the Kingdom of Mand, the girls in white trousers, the boys in long kilts, warlike and archaic. They spoke of their hopes. 'We in Mand are so very far from the Revolution that maybe we are near it,' said one of the girls, wistful and smiling: 'The Circle of Life!' and she showed the extremes meeting, in the circle of her slender, dark-skinned fingers. Amai and Aevi served them white wine and brown bread, the hospitality of the House. But the visitors, unpresumptuous, all rose to take their leave after barely half an hour. 'No, no, no,' Laia said, 'stay here, talk with Aevi and Amai. It's just that I get stiff sitting down, you see, I have to change about. It has been so good to meet you, will you come back to see me, my little brothers and sisters, soon?' For her heart went out to them, and theirs to her, and she exchanged kisses all round, laughing, delighted by the

dark young cheeks, the affectionate eyes, the scented hair, before she shuffled off. She was really a little tired, but to go up and take a nap would be a defeat. She had wanted to go out. She would go out. She had not been alone outdoors since – when? Since winter! before the stroke. No wonder she was getting morbid. It had been a regular jail sentence. Outside, the streets, that's where she lived.

She went quietly out the side door of the House, past the vegetable patch, to the street. The narrow strip of sour city dirt had been beautifully gardened and was producing a fine crop of beans and ceëa, but Laia's eye for farming was unenlightened. Of course it had been clear that anarchist communities, even in the time of transition, must work towards optimal self-support, but how that was to be managed in the way of actual dirt and plants wasn't her business. There were farmers and agronomists for that. Her job was the streets, the noisy, stinking streets of stone, where she had grown up and lived all her life, except for the fifteen years in prison.

She looked up fondly at the façade of the House. That it had been built as a bank gave peculiar satisfaction to its present occupants. They kept their sacks of meal in the bomb-proof money-vault, and aged their cider in kegs in safe deposit boxes. Over the fussy columns that faced the street carved letters still read, 'National Investors and Grain Factors Banking Association'. The Movement was not strong on names. They had no flag. Slogans came and went as the need did. There was always the Circle of Life to scratch on walls and pavements where Authority would have to see it. But when it came to names they were indifferent, accepting and ignoring whatever they got called, afraid of being pinned down and penned in, unafraid of being absurd. So this best known and second oldest of all the cooperative Houses had no name except The Bank.

It faced on a wide and quiet street, but only a block away began the Temeba, an open market, once famous as a center for black-market psychogenics and teratogenics, now reduced to vegetables, secondhand clothes, and miserable sideshows. Its

crapulous vitality was gone, leaving only half-paralyzed al-
coholics, addicts, cripples, hucksters, and fifth-rate whores,
pawnshops, gambling dens, fortune-telling, body-sculptors, and
cheap hotels. Laia turned to the Temeba as water seeks its level.

She had never feared or despised the city. It was her country.
There would not be slums like this, if the Revolution pre-
vailed. But there would be misery. There would always be
misery, waste, cruelty. She had never pretended to be changing
the human condition, to be Mama taking tragedy away from
the children so they won't hurt themselves. Anything but. So
long as people were free to choose, if they chose to drink
flybane and live in sewers, it was their business. Just so long as
it wasn't the business of Business, the source of profit and the
means of power for other people. She had felt all that before
she knew anything; before she wrote the first pamphlet,
before she left Parheo, before she knew what 'capital' meant,
before she'd been farther than River Street where she played
rolltaggie kneeling on scabby knees on the pavement with the
other six-year-olds, she had known it: that she, and the other
kids, and her parents, and their parents, and the drunks and
whores and all of River Street, were at the bottom of something
– were the foundation, the reality, the source. But will you drag
civilization down into the mud? cried the shocked decent
people, later on, and she had tried for years to explain to them
that if all you had was mud, then if you were God you made it
into human beings, and if you were human you tried to make it
into houses where human beings could live. But nobody who
thought he was better than mud would understand. Now, water
seeking its level, mud to mud, Laia shuffled through the foul,
noisy street, and all the ugly weakness of her old age was at
home. The sleepy whores, their lacquered hair-arrangements
dilapidated and askew, the one-eyed woman wearily yelling her
vegetables to sell, the half-wit beggar slapping flies, these were
her countrywomen. They looked like her, they were all sad,
disgusting, mean, pitiful, hideous. They were her sisters, her
own people.

She did not feel very well. It had been a long time since she had walked so far, four or five blocks, by herself, in the noise and push and striking summer heat of the streets. She had wanted to get to Koly Park, the triangle of scruffy grass at the end of the Temeba, and sit there for a while with the other old men and women who always sat there, to see what it was like to sit there and be old; but it was too far. If she didn't turn back now, she might get a dizzy spell, and she had a dread of falling down, falling down and having to lie there and look up at the people come to stare at the old woman in a fit. She turned and started home, frowning with effort and self-disgust. She could feel her face very red, and a swimming feeling came and went in her ears. It got a bit much, she was really afraid she might keel over. She saw a doorstep in the shade and made for it, let herself down cautiously, sat, sighed.

Nearby was a fruit-seller, sitting silent behind his dusty, withered stock. People went by. Nobody bought from him. Nobody looked at her. Odo, who was Odo? Famous revolutionary, author of *Community, The Analogy,* etc., etc. She, who was she? An old woman with grey hair and a red face sitting on a dirty doorstep in a slum, muttering to herself.

True? Was that she? Certainly it was what anybody passing her saw. But was it she, herself, any more than the famous revolutionary, etc., was? No. It was not. But who was she, then?

The one who loved Taviri.

Yes. True enough. But not enough. That was gone; he had been dead so long.

'Who am I?' Laia muttered to her invisible audience, and they knew the answer and told it to her with one voice. She was the little girl with scabby knees, sitting on the doorstep staring down through the dirty golden haze of River Street in the heat of late summer, the six-year-old, the sixteen-year-old, the fierce, cross, dream-ridden girl, untouched, untouchable. She was herself. Indeed she had been the tireless worker and thinker, but a blood clot in a vein had taken that woman away from her. Indeed she had been the lover, the swimmer in the

midst of life, but Taviri, dying, had taken that woman away with him. There was nothing left, really, but the foundation. She had come home; she had never left home. 'True voyage is return.' Dust and mud and a doorstep in the slums. And beyond, at the far end of the street, the field full of tall dry weeds blowing in the wind as night came.

'Laia! What are you doing here? Are you all right?'

One of the people from the House, of course, a nice woman, a bit fanatical and always talking. Laia could not remember her name though she had known her for years. She let herself be taken home, the woman talking all the way. In the big cool common room (once occupied by tellers counting money behind polished counters supervised by armed guards) Laia sat down in a chair. She was unable just as yet to face climbing the stairs, though she would have liked to be alone. The woman kept on talking, and other excited people came in. It appeared that a demonstration was being planned. Events in Thu were moving so fast that the mood here had caught fire, and something must be done. Day after tomorrow, no, tomorrow, there was to be a march, a big one, from Old Town to Capitol Square – the old route. 'Another Ninth Month Uprising,' said a young man, fiery and laughing, glancing at Laia. He had not even been born at the time of the Ninth Month Uprising, it was all history to him. Now he wanted to make some history of his own. The room had filled up. A general meeting would be held here, tomorrow, at eight in the morning. 'You must talk, Laia.'

'Tomorrow? Oh, I won't be here tomorrow,' she said brusquely. Whoever had asked her smiled, another one laughed, though Amai glanced round at her with a puzzled look. They went on talking and shouting. The Revolution. What on earth had made her say that? What a thing to say on the eve of the Revolution, even if it was true.

She waited her time, managed to get up and, for all her clumsiness, to slip away unnoticed among the people busy with their planning and excitement. She got to the hall, to the stairs, and began to climb them one by one. 'The general strike,' a

voice, two voices, ten voices were saying in the room below, behind her. 'The general strike,' Laia muttered, resting for a moment on the landing. Above, ahead, in her room, what awaited her? The private stroke. That was mildly funny. She started up the second flight of stairs, one by one, one leg at a time, like a small child. She was dizzy, but she was no longer afraid to fall. On ahead, on there, the dry white flowers nodded and whispered in the open fields of evening. Seventy-two years and she had never had time to learn what they were called.

THE WORLD'S GREATEST SCIENCE FICTION AUTHORS NOW AVAILABLE IN PANTHER BOOKS

Ursula K LeGuin

Orsinian Tales	75p ☐
The Wind's Twelve Quarters (*Volume 1*)	85p ☐
The Wind's Twelve Quarters (*Volume 2*)	75p ☐
The Dispossessed	95p ☐
The Left Hand of Darkness	75p ☐
The Lathe of Heaven	75p ☐
City of Illusions	75p ☐

Robert Silverberg

Earth's Other Shadow	75p ☐
A World Inside	75p ☐
Tower of Glass	60p ☐
Recalled to Life	50p ☐
A Time of Changes	50p ☐
Invaders from Earth	80p ☐
Master of Life and Death	75p ☐

J G Ballard

The Crystal World	75p ☐
The Drought	80p ☐
The Disaster Area	95p ☐
Vermilion Sands	60p ☐
Crash	95p ☐
High-Rise	60p ☐

THE WORLD'S GREATEST SCIENCE FICTION AUTHORS NOW AVAILABLE IN PANTHER BOOKS

Ray Bradbury

Fahrenheit 451	80p ☐
The Small Assassin	50p ☐
The October Country	50p ☐
The Illustrated Man	60p ☐
The Martian Chronicles	85p ☐
Dandelion Wine	95p ☐
The Golden Apples of the Sun	75p ☐
Something Wicked This Way Comes	75p ☐
The Machineries of Joy	60p ☐
Long After Midnight	95p ☐
The Best of Ray Bradbury Gift Set	£3.40 ☐

Keith Roberts

The Grain Kings	65p ☐
The Chalk Giants	75p ☐
Machines and Men	50p ☐
Pavane	40p ☐

Philip K Dick

Flow My Tears, The Policeman Said	80p ☐
Do Androids Dream of Electric Sheep?	75p ☐
Our Friends from Frolix 8	60p ☐
Now Wait for Last Year	85p ☐
Clans of the Alphane Moon	50p ☐
Zap Gun	75p ☐
The Three Stigmata of Palmer Eldritch	85p ☐
The Penultimate Truth	95p ☐
A Scanner Darkly	95p ☐
Ubik	75p ☐

THE WORLD'S GREATEST SCIENCE FICTION AUTHORS NOW AVAILABLE IN PANTHER BOOKS

Poul Anderson

Fire Time	75p ☐
Orbit Unlimited	60p ☐
Long Way Home	50p ☐
The Corridors of Time	50p ☐
Time and Stars	50p ☐
After Doomsday	50p ☐
Star Fox	40p ☐
Trader to the Stars	35p ☐

Philip José Farmer

The Stone God Awakens	80p ☐
Time's Last Gift	50p ☐
Traitor to the Living	85p ☐
To Your Scattered Bodies Go	85p ☐
The Fabulous Riverboat	85p ☐
Strange Relations	35p ☐
The Dark Design	£1.25 ☐

A E van Vogt

The Undercover Aliens	50p ☐
Rogue Ship	75p ☐
The Mind Cage	75p ☐
Slan	75p ☐
Moonbeast	85p ☐
The Voyage of the Space Beagle	75p ☐
The Book of Ptath	75p ☐
The War Against the Rull	70p ☐
Away and Beyond	75p ☐
Destination Universe!	75p ☐
Planets For Sale	75p ☐

ISAAC ASIMOV, GRAND MASTER OF SCIENCE FICTION – NOW AVAILABLE IN PANTHER BOOKS

The Left Hand of the Electron (Non-Fiction)	75p	☐
The Stars in their Courses (Non-Fiction)	60p	☐
Buy Jupiter!	75p	☐
The Gods Themselves	80p	☐
The Early Asimov *Volume 1*	60p	☐
The Early Asimov *Volume 2*	50p	☐
The Early Asimov *Volume 3*	75p	☐
The Early Asimov Gift Set	£1.75	☐
Earth is Room Enough	75p	☐
The Stars Like Dust	75p	☐
The Martian Way	50p	☐
Foundation	75p	☐
Foundation and Empire	75p	☐
Second Foundation	75p	☐
The Foundation Trilogy Gift Set	£1.75	☐
The Currents of Space	75p	☐
Nightfall One	75p	☐
Nightfall Two	75p	☐
The End of Eternity	75p	☐
I, Robot	75p	☐
The Caves of Steel	75p	☐
The Rest of the Robots	75p	☐

All these books are available at your local bookshop or newsagent, or can be ordered direct from the publisher. Just tick the titles you want and fill in the form below.

Name ..

Address ...

...

Write to Panther Cash Sales, PO Box 11, Falmouth, Cornwall TR10 9EN.

Please enclose remittance to the value of the cover price plus:

UK: 25p for the first book plus 10p per copy for each additional book ordered to a maximum charge of £1.05.

BFPO and EIRE: 25p for the first book plus 10p per copy for the next 8 books, thereafter 5p per book.

OVERSEAS: 40p for the first book and 12p for each additional book. *Granada Publishing reserve the right to show new retail prices on covers, which may differ from those previously advertised in the text or elsewhere.*